THE STORY BEHIND THE STORIES

---

12 DARK TALES AND THEIR PUBLISHERS

ANGELIQUE FAWNS

*This book is dedicated to all the hardworking publishers taking the
time and effort to help make writer's dreams come true.*

CONTENTS

Preface — vii

1. Ellery Queen Mystery Magazine — 1
2. Three Calendars — 9
3. Jolly Horror Press — 23
4. Inked — 29
5. Flying Ketchup Press — 39
6. The Versa Vice — 47
7. Soteira Press — 63
8. The Rougarou — 69
9. Pulp Modern — 79
10. A Time To Forget — 85
11. Czykmate Productions — 103
12. Death Metal Fan — 109
13. NBH Publishing — 121
14. The Midlife Storm — 129
15. Battle Goddess Productions — 137
16. A Tasty Festival — 145
17. Corona Books UK — 153
18. The Last Ride — 159
19. Nocturnal Sirens Publishing — 167
20. A Bug in Amber Alert — 173
21. Twisted Wing Productions — 175
22. Personal Demons — 181
23. The Gateway Review — 195
24. Planet Nine — 199
25. Bonus Story — 209
26. Farmyard Follies — 215

Acknowledgments — 221
About the Author — 223
Also by Angelique Fawns — 225

PREFACE

~

"If you want to be a writer, you must do two things above all others: read a lot and write a lot. There's no way around these two things that I'm aware of, no shortcut."
Stephen King

~

You've decided you want to write and sell your short stories?

It's on your bucket list; something planned for a mythical future when you have more time, or that old chestnut slurred about after too many cocktails.

"I'm going to become a writer."

Folks talk about climbing Mount Everest, but how many actually do it?

The same goes for selling your writing. How many aspiring authors successfully make sales? There is no magic spell (no matter what some fantasy stories promise). It takes time tapping on the keyboard, a thick skin to rejection, and the willingness to learn.

My journey began in 2018. I had a few false starts and eventually found success with more than 30 stories published in anthologies, magazines and on-line. This book will help you avoid some of the pitfalls, inspire you to keep trying and give you some actionable advice.

Unlike other guides on the market, this book goes directly to the source featuring one-on-one interviews with the publishers and editors who are buying stories in today's market. Get the inside scoop from the people behind the magazine and anthology covers.

It's not an easy road.

I currently have more than 500 rejections. Let's do some math here, with 30 stories published, that's a pick-up rate of 6%.

The number one thing successful writers have in common? They don't quit when someone tells them "No."

Carrie by Stephen King was rejected by over 30 publishers.

Agatha Christie started her career to a stream of rejections.

Judy Blume says on her website, "For two years I received nothing but rejections."

Yet, not all rejections are created equally. Some editors take the time to give useful advice and these tidbits are invaluable. This book also contains the best (and worst) rejections from my submissions.

My personal favorite was from an editor who told me, *"the piece made no sense."*

Then there was this more helpful piece of advice, *"we felt that the concept behind "A Deadful Friday the 13th" was engaging! That being said, the execution could have been better. Some sentences were a bit awkward and your descriptors could have been chosen with more care. More attention might also be given to the believability of the dialogue (for instance, a gang member probably wouldn't say, "I'm gonna get my gang members after that biotch").*

The editors at *Novel Noctule Literary Magazine* were right. My dialogue was terrible. I've made strides since then in creating more believable characters and conversation.

While working with editors and dealing with rejection, I developed a curiosity about the people behind the publications. Who are these wonderful people giving new authors a voice? Are they making any money? Why did they choose my story out of the hundreds submitted to them?

After a lucky request from *Ellery Queen Mystery Magazine* to write a blog post for them, I crafted a piece attempting to answer these questions.

A Conversation with Indie Anthology and Magazine Publishers

I interviewed a few of the editors who'd picked up my stories and their enthusiastic response was overwhelming. So many interesting answers! There was no way one blog post could fit it all.

I asked Stuart Conover at horrortree.com if he would be interested in posting interviews with publishers and he agreed. Daniel Scott White of Mythaxis.com also posts some of my interviews and articles on his website.

My background is in journalism and I've been writing non-fiction articles for years. My passion is writing strange stories. This book is the result of taking the skills I've been using for decades and combining them with my dream to write speculative fiction. I hope my journey can help yours.

ELLERY QUEEN MYSTERY MAGAZINE

hree Calendars

~

First published: November 2019
   Ellery Queen Mystery Magazine
   November/December 2019 issue
   Genre: Mystery
   Publisher/Editor: Janet Hutchings
   Pay: $250 US
   Previous rejections of Three Calendars: 2
   Rejections of others stories by EQMM: 1

∽

Ellery Queen Mystery Magazine

∽

A copy of this mystery magazine was always sitting on my mother's bedside table growing up, and I started reading it in my early teens. EQMM has been around since 1941 and has been cited as "the finest periodical of its kind" by *The Readers Encyclopedia of American Literature.* They pay professional rates and have had short stories from famous authors in many editions. Writers like William Faulkner, Agatha Christie, Ian Rankin, Val McDermid, Ruth Rendell and Peter Robinson have been featured. Charlaine Harris is one of my favourite authors, (I have every book in the *True Blood* series), and my story was in the same issue as her action-packed tale, "A Little Happy Hunting."

Their website proclaims they are the "winner of more than 100 major awards, including 22 Edgars from the Mystery Writers of America, EQMM is the most celebrated mystery and crime-fiction publication in the world."

So far, EQMM has been my biggest and most exciting sale.

∽

How "Three Calendars" found a home in *Ellery Queen Mystery Magazine*

∽

THE LACK of success at the beginning of my writing career helped me crack this market. EQMM has a feature in every issue called "Department of First Stories." This is a feature in all their editions which showcases an undiscovered talent. I submitted "Three Calendars" to EQMM in November 2018.

On February 21, 2019 I received this email from Janet Hutchings: "Thanks for letting us see 'Three Calendars.' EQMM is trying to determine whether you are eligible for our Department of First Stories. You mentioned a couple of previous fiction publications: Did you receive payment for them? Have you ever been paid for your fiction?"

My only success in the fiction market before this point was "Planet Nine" in *The Gateway Review* for no pay, so I explained that I had never received payment for any fiction story to date. By the time "Three Calendars" actually made it to print, my story "Death Metal Fan" was also up on haunt-edlmtl.com but the pay was only $2.

The introduction to "Three Calendars" in the actual issue read, "Angelique Fawns is a producer and writer for Global TV in Toronto, and a freelance agricultural reporter. She started writing fiction last summer and has already received honourable mentions in the Writers of the Future contest and Literary Taxidermy. Two of her stories have appeared online; this is her first paid publication."

Having a story in EQMM not only gave me a good pro market to list in my mini bio, but it was the genesis of this guide/anthology.

I received another email from Janet Hutchings on Friday September 27, "With your story coming out in the issue that goes on sale late in October, I wondered if you'd like to do a post for EQMM's blog site. The site is at www.somethingisgo-ingtohappen.net. A piece goes up there once a week, on

Wednesday. About once a month, I do it. The other spots are taken by authors, translators, scholars of the mystery, and others in the business. The topic could be anything you like as long as it relates to mystery fiction in some way."

I agreed to contribute, but then a cold dread swept over me. What could I possibly write that would be strong enough for EQMM? I started experiencing "imposter" syndrome. I read through the beautifully written blog posts by other authors and wasn't sure how I could contribute. I lost hours of sleep trying to figure out how to write an article good enough for the famous and long-lived EQMM! Unable to decide, I sent Hutchings a list of possible topics and she chose "a look at the day jobs and motivations behind small press anthology publishers."

While sending my stories out to market-after-market, I wondered about the people behind the open calls. Who were these individuals giving writers a chance to see their stories online and in print? Or in the case of podcasts, hear them? Were they making any money? While waiting for EQMM to publish my first paid fiction piece, a few more markets accepted my stories and I was beginning to make contacts.

I interviewed almost every editor/publisher who'd accepted my work to that point, and got some interesting answers. I was only able to use a small amount of it in my blog post for EQMM.

A Conversation With Indie Anthology and Magazine Publishers

I find most of my "open calls" at horrortree.com and love reading the interviews and extra content on the site. I contacted them and asked if they would be interested in the full interviews. Horrortree is Stuart Conover's brain child and he was enthusiastic about accepting my pieces. He warned he was not able to pay for articles right away, but there might be money in the future if Patreon picks up. (Now, I get about $5 US for each article.) In the process, I have discovered an amazing group of contributors. We have a private Facebook group and I love seeing how the calls for submissions are found and vetted.

The EQMM blog post started a new avenue of writing for me that uses my journalism background and my interest in the speculative fiction market.

Inspiration for "Three Calendars"

THERE IS someone close to me who is going through some cognitive decline, but is still highly functional in her daily life. It's fascinating to see how she battles short term memory lapses. It involves three calendars...

Lessons Learned

1) DON'T SELF-REJECT. I never imagined one of my first pick-ups would be from a pro-market publication. Stories sitting in dusty drawers, or long forgotten folders on your computer, will never find a home. Submit, submit, submit...

2) Be open to where your path goes. Freelance journalism

writing is nothing new to me. I'd been doing it for over 20 years. My dream is to become a "fiction" writer. Who knew my short story passion could intersect with my past experience in such a serendipitous way?

~

REJECTIONS

~

A**LLEGORY** M**AGAZINE**

"Dear Angelique,

Thank you for sharing your story with us. This was a really beautiful story. I love the way you tell this mystery within the context of your character's dementia. I don't know if it has quite enough of a speculative element, but I'm going to forward it on for further review by our editor. Congrats on making it to the next stage!"

T**HEN** I **RECEIVED THIS ONE**...

"A**NGELIQUE** -

I hate writing this letter.

I deeply regret to inform you that "Three Calendars" did not make the final cut for Volume 35/62 of ALLEGORY. Please understand that we received nearly 600 submissions for this issue and narrowed that down to only 54 finalists. ALL of those finalists are strong, quality stories - any of which we would be pleased and honored to publish. The final list of twelve is made by comparing the stories, more with an eye toward issue balance than the merits of one story over another. Your tale is a GREAT piece, and I'm very very sorry that we can't use it. For whatever it may be worth, we would like to include your name and the title of your story in the Honorable Mentions section of our mainpage.

Feel free to use this as a recommendation of your work to other markets. Again, my apologies. And good luck with your writing efforts."

2

THREE CALENDARS

$\mathcal{M}$y life is full of mysteries. Mysteries and calendars. A calendar by my bed, one on the fridge and one on my iPhone.

Opening my eyes, I start every day the same way. Birds chirp outside my window, light filters through my window, and I whisper to myself.

"My name is Betty. I'm a retired racehorse groom. And my sister is missing." I know these things. What I don't know is what day it is. Rolling out of bed I look at the calendar on my bedside table. Before I go to bed at night the first thing I do is X-out the current day. This way when I wake up and look at the calendar I can see right away that today is Sunday, September 30.

Looking beside me in the bed, I notice that there is an indent on the pillow next to me, but the body that should be lying there is missing. My husband. Where is the guy on a Sunday morning? It's not like he's a church goer. It seems I see less and less of him these days.

I pull the sheets up on the bed so it resembles something

neat and walk into my kitchen. It's not neat in there. My husband has left a mess. Toast crumbs everywhere, a dirty plate in front of the TV with last night's sports highlights playing on mute and a sludgy half-filled coffee.

I feel a familiar rise of frustration. Twenty-some-odd years married and the guy can't figure out how to put a cup into the dishwasher? Argh. I carry the offending things to the sink and grab my own mug and start a coffee for myself in the Keurig. My reflection stares back at me from the window, distracting me from the lovely view out there. At 59, I still look pretty good. My auburn hair curls around my face with only a bit of gray sprinkled at the temples. My cheek bones are still striking, not covered yet by the slow spread of weight that gets most of us in old age. It seems the pounds are finding me from the bottom up. My thighs and hips are heavier, but my chest is still boy flat with defined collar bones peeking out from my nightgown.

What was I doing? There is a coffee cup decorated with a horse in my hand that says *I've spent most my life in the saddle, the rest I've just wasted.* That's right, I was making a cup of Keurig's Krispy Kreme coffee. I love the convenience but hate the guilt. I remember a meme I saw on Facebook of all these little used pods encircling the planet in space. Destroying the earth one caffeine hit at a time. Why can't I forget that horrible picture when I can't seem to remember what I planned today?

Good thing I have another handy calendar for that. Taking my coffee and sipping at it, I wander over to the fridge to look at the photocopied calendar given to me every month by my son with my grandchild's schedule on it. It's Sunday, September 30, and the day is wide open. I don't have to pick up my grandson after school today. That is my biggest responsibility these days. Providing a shuttle service and daycare for five-year-old Jack. Both his parents work and need an hour or two before they can pick him up at the end of the day.

This gives me plenty of time to look for Elvie. When I try and talk to my husband Paul? -Phil? -yes, Phil, about how I'm worried about her he gets belligerent.

"Betty! Elvie is dead. Please please let this go," he always says, putting his hands on his blonde balding head in exasperation. Then he walks away and turns on the sports channel or locks himself in his office.

I also know what I heard, and it's not too late. That phone call a couple weeks ago? -I am sure it was just a couple weeks,- whenI heard her plea for help:

"Betty, he's got me trapped. You've got to help me. He's going to kill me this time, I am sure of it. I'm running out of..." Then a gasp and nothing. Before I could find out where she was, the connection was lost.

Still, I shouted "Elvie! Elvie! What has the bastard done to you?! Elviiiiee?"

Nothing but the hum of empty space.

Elvie, at only sixteen, had married the devil. He was charming and handsome and had whisked her right off her feet. Johnny Harvey was the son of the local Uncles of Anarchy biker gang and when he saw beautiful Elvie rollerblading around the neighbourhood, he decided he had to have her. Her luminous skin, long blonde hair swinging to her bum, and grey-green eyes. She was stunning, naïve and had no idea about biker-gang culture.

I was the elder sister by three years and knew that the Harvey family was suspected in several robberies in the area, dealt drugs, and might even be implicated in a few murders. I warned her, this guy is bad news. His aspiration was to be a career criminal and join the same biker gang his dad ran. But Elvie was smitten. Johnny was like the birds with broken wings she brought home and the stray cats she tried to convince our mother to let her keep. She was sure he could be saved. So, one day she rode off on the back of his bike and officially became Johnny's girl.

I see a yellow sticky note at the bottom of my calendar. It says, *Look in your day planner. It is in your purse.* Still sipping my coffee, I try to remember where my purse is. Looking around, I can't see it and can't remember where I put it. I feel a swell of panic start to roll up in my chest. It's a familiar feeling. Lately, I need to get more sleep or eat more greens. It's getting harder to remember things, but I don't have the Alzheimer's or dementia or any other of those brain diseases. My obnoxious daughter-in-law is constantly telling me that I need to go see a doctor about my memory. How dare she? I am fine. Everyone forgets things now and then. She should go see a doctor about her rudeness problem.

My boss at work had a rudeness problem. He accused me of messing up my best racehorse's medication and suggested I retire. I know I didn't screw up. Colic can happen at anytime to a horse. And he recovered. It's not like he died. Of course, it wasn't really a suggestion from my boss, so I ended up retiring earlier than I wanted to.

Looking back at my fridge calendar I see a little yellow sticky note on the calendar. *Look in your day planner. It is in your purse.* A logical place for a purse is on the shelf beside the coat hanger.

Walking down the hall to front door I see it is there and take my purse back to the kitchen table. It is a lovely item with soft brown leather and fringe tassels hanging from it. I have good taste. Sitting down, I pull my day planner out and open it up to where the little marker indicates. On Saturday, September 29, I wrote *Checked out Uncles of Anarchy Clubhouse. No Elvie. Maybe marijuana fields?*

Wow. I am one old bold bitch. Did I really go check out the Uncles of Anarchy clubhouse yesterday? Those guys are dangerous. But I must have. I scrunch up my nose and try hard to remember. But nothing comes to me. The day planner/bible says I did go there, and I have learned to trust my own notes. Every day for the month of September shows I checked out all Elvie's past addresses and usual haunts, but had no luck finding her. I can see my search clearly in front of me. Every detail of my sleuthing as I look for Elvie.

The run-down trailer she lived in with Johnny 20 minutes from us. The nail salon/massage parlour she worked at is in town. Her favorite pool bar where lots of the bikers' "old ladies" hung out, is there too. No one had seen her.

Elvie moved out soon after she started dating Johnny. When my father found out Johnny and some of his wanna-be biker friends were hiding stolen goods in our garage, it was like a nuclear bomb went off. That day is etched in my memory. Dad went ballistic. He shouted and swore and threatened to call the cops. Elvie was crying. I was crying. My mom was crying. But that was it for Dad. He believed in following the law and keeping your nose clean. Johnny had to come get his "stolen shit" out immediately and Elvie had to leave her good-for-nothing criminal boyfriend or get the hell out of his house.

Elvie called Johnny who showed up with one of those non-descript white vans and loaded up the seventeen TVs he'd stashed in our garage and muttered something about how we better not call the cops or else. My Dad's face went so purple I thought he was going to have a heart attack on the spot. Elvie dashed up to her room to quickly pack a bag and then ran back outside and hopped into the van.

"No! Elvie, this is a terrible mistake! Mom, Dad you can't let her go! Please stop her! Elvie!" I remember crying and shouting.

But my parents had done nothing. I guess even if they had forced her to stay that day, she would have just run off later. She was crazy smitten with that loser. Johnny had taken Elvie and his TV's off in that white van and I only saw her once after that. My sister had joined the world of criminals. I was my father's daughter and also believed in following the law and keeping my nose clean. I told Elvie if she was going to stay with a guy who lived an illegal, immoral life, I didn't want to see her again until she was ready to leave him.

I think she almost got away. Ten years later she showed up at my home in the early afternoon. Phil and I had been married for a while then and he was still at work. As a racehorse groom, I used to nip home for a nap between the morning feed/exercising chores and racing later that day. If you drew a late race on the card, you could be working till one A.M. in the morning bedding your horse back down and putting on bandages and poultices. It was just luck I was home that day.

"Betty, Betty, you've got to help me," she said as she tried to cover up a black eye with her long hair. "He's going to kill me one of these days!" There was no hiding the bloody lip. Her words were slurred because of it. The years had been hard on her. She had lost her luminous glow and looked older than I did.

"God! We've got to call the cops Elvie. You can live with

me! I should get you to the hospital!" I blurted, shouting over my shoulder while I ran to the kitchen to get some ice.

"No! If you call the cops, he will kill the both of us for sure. Oh Jesus. I can't believe this is my life. I'm not his wife, I'm his personal punching bag. And I don't even want to tell you what he has me doing at that filthy massage parlour," Elvie said, sobbing into the ice and paper towel.

I was trying to convince her to at least let me drive her to the hospital, not being able to process what she had said about the massage parlour quite yet, when there was a banging on my front door.

"Oh god," Elvie said, starting to tremble. "It's him. I've got to go." Her eyes went deadpan and the tears cleared up as she heaved a big sigh.

"No! No, you are not going with him," I said as I stomped to the door. There was a bat sitting there that Phil had placed "just in case a bear comes a-knockin'". I picked it up and swung the door open.

Johnny was standing there with a bottle of wine and flowers in his hand.

"Get lost! Elvie doesn't want to see you! Bastard!" I said, hoisting the bat over my head.

He ignored me. "Elvie honey, I love you more than my Harley, more than any other of those girls, you got to come home with me. I'm nothing without you. I promise to be better!"

I swung the bat at his head, but he caught it with the hand not holding gifts for my sister.

"Easy there, or I may have to take you over my knee" he said to me with a dark chuckle.

"Next time I am not going for your head. I am going for your balls!" I said, struggling to get my bat out of his hand. I was going to have to go to the gym or maybe buy a big attack dog. Johnny was not going to come to my house again and get away unscathed. I don't care what kind of patch he wears on his jacket.

"Betty, stop it honey. I am going to go home with him," Elvie said, coming out from the kitchen. "Johnny you had better not touch my sister. But I will come home with you."

"No! We will call the cops! I'll call Phil! You don't have to go with him!" I said, desperately tugging on her arm as she walked past me out the door. I was still also trying to get my bat back from Johnny's leather clad arm.

"Promise not to hit me with that bat so I can hug my girl?" Johnny said, looking triumphant. He let go of the bat and put that arm around Elvie's shoulders.

She slumped in resignation and the both of them walked back to his bike parked in my driveway. He stowed the flowers and wine in a saddle bag. She avoided my eyes as she climbed onto the back of the black Harley-Davidson. I hated those stupid bikes. I'd seen my sister whisked away from me on that ugly noisy machine.

That was the last time I ever saw her.

Shaking the memory of her blonde hair blowing out behind her as they drove away, I go back to looking at the day planner. "Marijuana fields" is written on today. I remember Elvie showing me where the Uncles of Anarchy grew a bunch of their plants when we were hiking in one of the regional forests. This was before Dad kicked her out of the house and her relationship was still new.

I get up to grab a muffin from the counter and look out my back window. As I nibbled on it I try to remember where the corn field was. The group of plants had been subtly inserted in the middle of an unsuspecting farmer's crop.

There was a shed not too far from the pot-growing area that Elvie had giggled about having sex in with Johnny. Those early days when she was madly in love with her bad boy. Maybe he had taken a much older Elvie back there, beaten her up, and stashed her in the shed?

Yes, I'll check the shed today. But how am I going to get there? Not knowing exactly where that farmer's field was in the public forest could mean hours walking. And my old legs aren't as spry as they used to be. A bit of Planter's fasciitis here... a bit of arthritis there.

Taking another bite of my muffin, I gaze out the window at the pastoral beauty. We had been lucky to find a small acreage close to Phil's job as a supervisor at a local quarry and less than an hour from the racetrack. When I retired a couple years ago, I took Ducky, one of the racing thoroughbred geldings I was grooming from the track with me. He had blown out his tendon at his last race, and his owner/trainer knew he would never race again. Rather than put him into the retired racehorse program, I convinced them to let me bring him home. I had a small fenced field out behind our house and wouldn't mind something to fuss over to fill my days. I had rubbed four racehorses for my trainer and back then my brain was always full of exercise schedules, feed requirements and special tack assignments. I was very proud of how I could keep every thoroughbred's different needs straight in my brain. As soon as I stopped working, it was like I lost my edge. I did not start slipping while I was at the track, my boss is wrong about that. I did not get that horse's medication wrong. But my brain did retire right along with me and decided it didn't need to hold information the same way.

What was I planning to do with Ducky again? I go back to look at my day planner and see that I wanted to go look for that farmer's shed near the pot field. Because Elvie is missing and in trouble! Grabbing my keys, purse (making sure I put my day planner back in it), and a warm jacket, I walk out of the back door and hop into my pickup truck. It already has the horse trailer attached to it and I keep my saddle and bridle in it at all times.

Walking out into the field with a lead shank and apple treat, I grab Ducky and walk him to the trailer. Like a good boy he jumps right on and we are off to ride in the regional forest. Wow. I can sure handle a horse trailer well. A small bloom of pride wells up in me. If you do an action enough times, there are some things you never forget!

Every time I had a day off at the race track I used to ride my old mare Tulip on the trails. As soon as my husband and I bought our hobby farm, I purchased Tulip from a trail riding barn and financed this little trailer. Sadly, she died a couple years ago from old age, and I had been horseless at home until I retired with Ducky. My feet and hands automatically drive me to the trailhead entrance.

What a gorgeous day for a hack! The sun is shining and the fall air is crisp. I can see some of the leaves in the forest have changed making a colourful canopy to ride under. Before I get out of the truck, I take a pen from my purse and write on the back of my hand.

FIND THE SHED BY THE POT FIELD. LOOK FOR ELVIE.

Sometimes I get lost in the beauty of the paths and ride for hours with my brain happy and free of thoughts. Now, I need to focus and make sure I finish my mission. Elvie could be in serious trouble. This reminder on my hand will keep me on track. Grabbing my helmet, I strap it on. Safety first, right? Even my old head needs protection.

I throw my saddle on Ducky, slip the bridle over his ears and he stands with patience as I balance on the wheel well to launch myself onto his back. For an ex-racehorse he is a surprisingly lovely ride. He snorts and shakes his chestnut head and starts to walk eagerly along the dirt path.

When we hit a wider sand stretch I let him move into a controlled gallop and two of us seem united in our glee. The trees brush by quickly and I can feel his muscles tensing and releasing beneath me. What a rush. This is my favorite thing to do. My love of horses had taken me to my career at the racetrack, but riding is my true passion. I could do this all day. When the path narrows again, I pull Ducky up and lean forward to give him a pat.

FIND THE SHED BY THE POT FIELD. LOOK FOR ELVIE is written in pen on my hand. Right! Enough messing around on the trails, I have to go save my sister. I know this trail will lead to the edge of the forest and the farmer's corn field.

Everything is quiet and the only thing I can hear is the huffing from Ducky's breath as he picks his way along the narrow path. Soon we come out to the edge and I see that the silage crop has already been harvested. This will make it much easier to get to the shed on the other side of the private property. Tall corn is a bugger to ride through. We walk along the edge of the cedar rail fencing until I find the break in. It was probably made by bikers so they could access their illegal crop hidden in the legal one. Ducky pushes his way through the opening and I urge him into a trot when I see the shed way over on the other edge of the property.

Hopefully no one is out hunting on the land today. It's getting to that time of year when the deer tags came out. And Ducky is sort of like a tall orange deer. After a few minutes, I come to the shed and hop off my horse. Because there's grass surrounding the dilapidated wood structure, I unhook one rein from his bridle and let him eat while I tie the other end of the rein to a stirrup.

Walking cautiously up to the shed, I try to hear if anyone is struggling inside.

"Elvie? Are you in there? Elvie? It's Betty," I whisper loudly.

I walk up to the door, which is precariously latched with a bit of rusty wire, and I open it. Peering into the depths, I can't see anything, so I take a careful step inside. The shed is empty. The faint smell of old garbage and the more recent smell of skunk tickles my nose. A few beer bottles and the ends of weed joints sit on the ground, covered by the grime of passing time. Taking a deep breath, I can see Elvie is not here. I don't know whether to be relived or disappointed.

Someone has scratched a message on the wall with a knife in the old wood.

Betty, this is a note from yourself. If you are reading this you need to know Elvie is dead. You did find her here. A year ago. You were too late. Johnny killed her, but because you called in the cops they convicted him for murder and he is in jail. You don't have to look anymore.

I gasp and fall to my knees in the dirt on the floor. Tears started sliding down my face. It's hard to breath, but I concentrate and count to ten and try to slow down every intake of oxygen. Elvie is dead. My beautiful sister was killed by that rabid bastard. I hope he rots in jail. I hope he's gang raped in the shower twice a day. I hope.... I just can't believe she is gone. Using the back of my sleeve to wipe away my tears, I stumble out of the shed and try to get back on Ducky.

There's nothing to stand on, so it's hard to haul my old

bones and big bottom back onto his back but I manage. Sniffling and in shock I ride back to the trailer. Elvie is dead? I had already found her? I have a vague memory of her blond hair tinged with red. The rope on her wrists... but most of it is a blur. Ducky jumps right back on the trailer and I drive home. I watch the sun setting as I pull into my driveway. The red and purples reflect the bleeding in my heart. The memory of blood in Elvie's hair.

Ducky is happy to go back to eating grass in his field and I know he has plenty of water in his trough. I walk into the house, trying to not to sob, and see Phil sitting on the couch. He has a bottle of scotch in front of him and a big tumbler full of ice. Most of the bottle of scotch is empty. He is probably a few drinks in. As usual.

"Betty! I saw the trailer and Ducky was gone so I went ahead and made some dinner. There is a plate in the microwave for you. How was your ride?" Phil asks, his speech already slurring and eyes out of focus.

A wave of anger washes over me. No sense in trying to talk him now about Elvie. If he isn't ignoring me and locked in his office, he's three sheets to the wind. When I retired, he started indulging his fondness for single malt. When I try and have a decent conversation with him, he complains I tell all the same stories over and over again. Don't we all? What else do old folks do? I can't bear to try and talk to him about Elvie when he's drunk. Ignoring him and his plate in the microwave, I have a quick shower and slip into my pajamas.

A deep exhaustion and depression rolls through my body. It's like the air has turned to molasses, and I fight my way through it. I need to go to bed. But first, I have to update my calendars. It is the end of the month. I wander out to the fridge, ignoring Phil, and put September in the garbage. My son has October ready to go with Jack's schedule. The second thing I do is flip my day planner over to October and put it back in my purse. All those empty boxes waiting to be filled. Next I go to the bedside table, take a pen and put a big X through Sunday, September 30, and flip that page to October. Tomorrow is Monday, October 1.

As soon as my head hits the pillow I fall into a deep sleep. I don't even hear Phil come to bed.

My life is full of mysteries. Mysteries and calendars. A calendar by my bed, one on the fridge and one on my iPhone.

Opening my eyes, I start every day the same way. Birds chirp outside my window, light filters through my window, and I whisper to myself.

"My name is Betty. I used to be a racehorse groom. And my sister is missing."

3

JOLLY HORROR PRESS

*I*nked

~

FIRST PUBLISHED: December 10, 2019
    Accursed
    Jolly Horror Press
    Genre: Horror/Comedy
    Publisher/Editor: Jonathan Lambert
    Pay: $25 US
    Previous rejections of Inked: 0
    Rejections of other stories by JHP: 3

∽

Jolly Horror Press

∽

JHP IS a small independent publishing house run by Jonathan Lambert, an engaging and approachable horror comedy aficionado. He lives just outside of Washington D.C. and I asked him what he did as a day job.

Lambert says, "Interesting question. Truth be told, I like to keep my day job separate from my role as publisher at Jolly Horror Press, and even my writing. In my experience, people sometimes begin to act odd or different once they find out a coworker writes or publishes horror. God forbid the little old lady a few offices away grabs one of our books and starts reading about incubi and witch orgies, or some other risqué story in one of these anthologies. She'd never look at me the same, or she'll never leave me alone. LOL. So, I'd rather avoid that all together If I can.

I'll tell you a little though. I'm a senior executive at a US Federal Government agency. I lead a very large program (~2.5 billion dollars) to modernize aging computer systems over the next ten years."

When asked why he created JHP, "The genre I write is horror/comedy. Short stories. The long days I put in at the office aren't very conducive to writing longer works at this time (maybe something I'll do when I retire.) For many years I would submit these stories to other anthologies. I had a good bit of success, yet horror/comedy stories are difficult to place. Most anthologies want pure horror. I also sold a lot of stories for peanuts. I think 3 dollars for a 5,000-word story was the lowest. I also noticed how so many publications no longer pay at all. They pay through 'exposure' but if they aren't well marketed, the exposure is limited.

After a few years of experience selling short stories to anthologies, I just decided that I could do a better job. Provide better customer service, and be more author friendly. I could also create a press that is dedicated to horror/comedy. Finally, these stories could have a home. I just needed the name, and one day Jolly Horror Press just popped in my head. The rest is history."

◠

How "Inked" found a home in *Accursed*

◠

One of the most auspicious finds during my struggle to get my first stories published was Lambert and JHP. He initially rejected the first two stories I submitted to his call for *Accursed*, a horror comedy anthology featuring 26 stories telling the tales of cursed items. However, instead of giving me a form rejection letter, he gave me a little bit of encouragement, which was all I needed.

He rejected my first story outright, a piece about a possessed bedroom fan and added on his rejection email, "Unfortunately we aren't going to accept "Death Metal Fan" for our Accursed antho. It's a fun story but doesn't fit the vibe for the book. Thanks again for submitting."

He called my story "fun", so I promptly sent him another piece I'd written about a Ferris Wheel haunted by ghosts. (See "The Last Ride" later in this collection.)

Lambert wrote, "Fun little story but not really a cursed item story in the sense we are looking for, so it doesn't really fit the theme. Sorry, but we won't take this one either. Hate to have to send you a second rejection. I do think you are a wonderful writer; your stories are written well, and I really appreciate that. This one just isn't right for the theme. We are still open until June 30."

I thought a possessed fan and haunted Ferris wheel were absolutely cursed items, so I tried to probe him about what he was looking for to fit his short story collection.

I wrote back, "I am going to take a third crack at this and I'm writing this one specifically for your anthology. What about a story featuring ink that when tattooed onto a person's body forces them to fall in love with the tattoo artist? Of course, things go terribly wrong... That would be an accursed item, yes? And hopefully you don't have a story like this yet?"

He replied, "We haven't accepted any cursed tattoo stories yet. We did get one or two, but they weren't good and didn't make the cut. So, sounds like a cool idea depending on how you pull it off."

I got to work writing "Inked" and tried to bend every stereotype I could to make the story surprising. I read the piece to a few of my friends and they giggled at my main character's love interest; a badass biker dude with an unexpected set of wheels.

I sent it off to JHP, and got this reply, "Angelique, I am really sorry to have to tell you this... Just kidding! We love "Inked", and would like to offer you a place in Accursed."

Finally! I had a story accepted by JHP. (Mini heart attack aside when I thought I was getting my third rejection.) Then came the editing process, which was also "unexpected" and an enormous learning experience. Of all the pieces I have penned, both fiction and non-fiction, no other editor has been as generous with his figurative red pen. Lambert edited the hell out of my story, even sending it to an actual tattoo artist to make sure I got all the minutiae of the art correct. (I had a few details wrong.)

I've since interviewed Lambert twice for horrortree.com, helping promote his anthologies and small press. He picked up a second story of mine for his *Coffin Blossoms* anthology, a collection of comedy horror stories without a specific theme. You will find that story and more about JHP in my next volume of "short stories plus interviews", *The Publishers Behind the Pages*.

PS. I was so impressed with Lambert's editing skills, I asked for his help proofreading this anthology.

~

INSPIRATION FOR "INKED"

~

LIKE MANY, I love the *Sons of Anarchy* television show. All those dark and dangerous bikers covered in tattoos. But what if a woman fell in love with a man she *thought* was a biker and he turned out to be something entirely different?

~

LESSONS LEARNED

~

1) ONE OF the number one rules in the short fiction market is, "Thou shalt not reply to rejections." However, in this instance the editor seemed open and encouraging so I took a chance and responded to the second rejection email. Sometimes persistence pays off.

2) Be open to revisions. Some pretty serious editing went into getting this story to final polish. As Dr. Seuss says, "So the writer who breeds more words than he needs, is making a chore for the reader who reads.

4

———

INKED

*H*er entire body was covered in art. Even with her employee discount at Taboo Tattoo, it had cost her a fortune. Hearts seeped rivulets of blood down her soft white arms, roses with sharp thorns decorated sturdy legs, black swans hugged her chest, and snakes slithered down her back. Lily was into bad boys, and thought she'd found her soulmate. He just didn't know it yet. Snake was only interested in her as his tattoo artist. She was losing sleep and going crazy dreaming of the big, heavily-tatted man with hypnotic eyes. There was nothing she wouldn't do to get him, including finding herself in a dodgy part of the city in the wee hours of the morning.

The shop was called Pagan Possibilities. It could only be accessed off an alley strewn with used needles in the Queen Street West area of Toronto. The shop had once been a garage, and still showed signs of it. Paint peeled from the aluminum siding, and a window was blacked out. The smell of cannabis hung in the air like long dead skunk. Lily clutched the shop's worn flyer in one sweaty hand, trying to summon up the courage to enter. She hoped this was the right place. The literature said the shop was only open from midnight till 3 a.m. on Friday nights, so she had hopped on a streetcar and braved drunks, hookers and opioid users to try her luck.

Fingering the stud in her lip, Lily took a deep breath, pushed open the door and walked in. Licorice incense tickled her nostrils. A low glow came from crystal lamps and candles and the décor could only be called hoarder-chic. Jars filled with murky liquid, candles, incense holders, garden gnomes, pentacles, hundreds of books, and bedazzled shawls fought for space on every dusty shelf and table. Lily picked up a jar, but quickly put it down again after seeing toad heads floating in the liquid.

"Hmm, there is something you desire. Something you want more than anything in the universe. You think I can help you," said a gravelly voice from the dark.

Lily saw a hunched figure in a dim corner of the garage behind a desk and started squeezing past overflowing tables. As her eyes adjusted to the gloom, she saw the proprietor of Pagan Possibilities wasn't hunch-backed, but wearing a set of wings and a positively stunning black lace gown.

"Hello darling! Look at you! Those are some amazing tattoos, and I positively love the purple hair. I'm Penny and this is my little shop of horrors and wonders," she said, one hand on a slender hip, the other twirling a piece of her long black wig.

Lily looked in astonishment at the store owner. She was gorgeous. A serpent-like body, muscular and sensuous, with soft dark eyes, and only the faint shadow of a beard on her face.

"I was at a summer solstice party with some of my Wiccan

friends and found this pamphlet. I'm desperately in love with a man who comes to my tattoo shop and my heart is gonna explode into a million bloody pieces if I can't have him," Lily said, pointing to a tattoo of a shattered heart on her forearm. "Like this."

"Well, you've come to the right place, I have some powerful potions, but if you're a tattoo artist, I have a really extraordinary ink. But let me warn you girl, once you needle this into someone's skin, they will be yours forever. Be sure or beware," Penny said as she reached beneath the desk and brought out a small container of scarlet liquid.

Lily looked in fascination at the iridescent red ink. It slowly swirled and curled in the clear plastic tube.

"It almost looks alive! I'll take it. How much?"

"Three hundred dollars, but make sure this is what you want," Penny cautioned.

Lily was already seducing Snake in her mind, and quickly counted out 300 dollars in large bills. She handed it to Penny as she tucked the ink into her pocket. Hustling out of there, she went back to her apartment above the tattoo shop to catch a few hours of sleep before her favorite client arrived at noon the next day.

WHEN SNAKE WALKED into the shop, sweat started to trickle down Lily's armpits. She was wearing her most flattering skull and crossbones mini dress, and had made a special effort to flat iron the long purple hair on the unshaven side of her head. Six feet tall, with a gym-toned body, long black hair caught back in a man bun, and startling green eyes, he was the most gorgeous human being on Earth. Luckily, he was addicted to ink, and came in at least once a month to get a new tat, or add some color to an older one.

"Hi Lily! I'm looking to add something special to my arm sleeve today. Maybe a dragon? A bloody sword?" Snake said.

He untucked his black t-shirt from his tight Levi's and pulled it off. Lily greedily drank in the wide back, taut muscles, and artistic ink covering most of his upper body. She had done most of the work, and a world of castles, dragons, swords and starships already decorated him.

"How about something special today? I designed this just for you," Lily showed him a drawing of a large skull whose teeth clenched a rose dripping blood from the petals.

"That's fantastic. Put it on my tab, and let's do it," he said as he settled into her chair.

Lily knew he was good for the cash so she took out her special tube of scarlet liquid and poured it into the ink cap. It came out in thick globs and looked like it was breathing as it pulsed in the gun. She found a clear place on his forearm and started working on his skin with the tattoo needles. Breathing in his smell of Irish Spring soap and sweat, butterflies started their familiar flapping in her belly. How many nights had she lain awake imagining her thighs wrapped around his motorcycle as she pressed her lips into his back? Then looking into his eyes over a bonfire as they sipped whiskey?

The hum of the machine masked her excited breathing as the black skull with the red rose appeared beneath her fingers. A tattoo of this size took her around four hours, but the minutes flew by. The longer she could be near Snake the better. She paid special attention to the flower, making sure the ink was extra vibrant. This tattoo was going to be the most important work of her life. After Lily carefully cleaned the reddened skin, she tried to put a bandage on it, but Snake flapped his hand at her.

"You know me baby, I live dangerously. Let it breath, "

Snake pulled his t-shirt back on and studied her for a minute, "you know, you look different today. Really beautiful. There is something... I don't know. Do you want to go for dinner with me tonight?"

"Yes," Lily gasped, that special ink worked fast. The skull on his arm seemed to wink at her and the blood streaming off the rose looked wet and alive.

"It's four now, what time do you want me to come get you? I almost don't feel like leaving you, I kinda want to just stay here and stare at you"

"Now! I can go now, you're my last client of the day, the benefits of being self-employed," Lily said, "let me grab my purse and we can get some pre-dinner cocktails."

She followed him out of the shop then locked the door behind her, unable to believe her luck. The newly created skull watched her from his arm. She shook her head, it must be an illusion. No tattoo was actually alive. Snake walked down the sidewalk and stopped at a touring bicycle locked to a metal post, with a helmet hanging off the handle bars.

Lily's jaw dropped, "I thought you said you rode a mean bike."

"Yes, this is a top-of-the-line Schwinn. Want me to double you? Or do you have your own wheels?" Snake said, flashing her his devastating grin. "You are gorgeous, those curves and that purple hair. I don't know how I didn't notice before!"

Lily stared at the five-speed, not sure what to say. This put a kink in her Sons of Anarchy fantasy.

"Here, climb up on the seat and I'll stand and peddle. I'll take you to my place. I got some beer in the fridge and we can figure out where to go for dinner," he said, looping one long leg over and leaning into the handle bars to make room for her.

She climbed up behind him and tried to enjoy holding onto his broad back as he push-pedaled them down the road. At least the guy was environmentally conscious. Though it was only about a ten-minute ride, her dress got wrinkled and her butt was sore when they showed up outside a small semi-detached brownstone. They both tumbled off the bike.

"Wait till you meet my Mom! You're going to love her. Hey, maybe she can make us dinner tonight and save some money?" Snake said walking quickly up the driveway after dumping his bike onto the lawn.

"You live with your mom still?" Lily asked as she hustled after him. "Aren't you like thirty-years-old?"

"Thirty-five actually. She's divorced and likes the company. Besides I'm between jobs right now, so it works for me," Snake pushed open the front door.

"How long have you been unemployed?"

"A couple years, but I'm working on an app. Hey Mom, come meet Lily! She's my tattoo artist!"

Lily followed him, noticing the photos of a young Snake (he definitely had a dorky, pimply stage), and crocheted art informing guests that "Hookers Do It With One Hand" and "I Crochet Past My Bedtime."

A grey-haired lady came out of the kitchen smiling, "Snake, I'm glad you've finally brought a girlfriend home! I was beginning to think you played for the other team."

"Mom, don't embarrass me. I'm taking Lily down to the basement okay? Maybe you can bring us down some snacks?" Snake said, turning to descend a narrow set of stairs.

"Nice meeting you," Lily said to the still grinning lady as she awkwardly followed Snake.

Getting to the bottom of the twisty stairs, she took in the Star Wars posters, big video game console, ratty couch with a 70's flower pattern and weight set in the corner. The smell of dirty gym socks and mildew was overpowering. Lily felt her heart sink. This wasn't quite how she envisioned her first romantic encounter with the man of her dreams.

Snake was leaning into a beer fridge and pulled out two bottles of Michelob Ultra. "Here you go Lily. Want to play some Mario Cart?" he asked, tossing one to her.

Lily twisted off the top and took a long guzzle. Maybe she could save this.

"Not big into video games, but I hear there's gonna be a rave on the beach tomorrow night. They're bringing in a DJ and everything," she said.

"Tomorrow? I can't. That's my Dungeons and Dragons night. You can come play with us if you like," Snake invited.

Lily stared at him. He played fantasy board games? Maybe she couldn't salvage this. He drank his beer in long swallows and the newly inked skull was laughing at her now. She had been picturing dinner in an exotic restaurant on King Street, with candles flickering as they supped oysters— knowing what that would lead to later. Not mom-made snacks in a man-boy's basement. Where were all his sexy friends who gave themselves tough nicknames?

"How did you get the name Snake?" she asked.

"Oh, my name is Stanley, but when I was younger, I was really good at Snakes & Ladders," he said plopping himself down on the filthy torn couch.

"So, Stanley, I'm gonna to have to get going. Sorry to cut this date short."

"Hey, when can I see you again? I go to my Cosplay Club on Sunday, I bet you'd fit right in," he said jumping to his feet, "do you need me to double you back on my bike?"

Lily was already walking up the stairs, but stopped, "Cosplay? What's that?"

"You dress up as really cool characters and act like them, sometimes make mini-plays. I never miss Comic-Con."

Lily blinked. She wouldn't be caught dead dressed up as a comic book character. She continued up the stairs and called over her shoulder, "No need for another bike ride, I'll catch a cab."

She could hear Stanley's mom in the kitchen, but slipped out the door without saying goodbye. Lily was disappointed, how did she read him so wrong? Tears streamed down her face as she walked down the driveway. Snake lived in his parent's basement, was unemployed, and played Dungeons and Dragons? And here she thought she was going to be a biker's "old lady." Lily wiped away her tears and started laughing. She stopped walking and had to hold on to a lamppost to keep herself up. She laughed and howled and then sunk to her bum leaning against the pole, completely drained.

After ordering an Uber she went home and fell into an exhausted sleep. For the first night in a long time, she did not dream of rolling around with a naked Snake.

THE NEXT DAY, Sunday, she had a group of five bridesmaids, along with the bride, come in to get matching ankle tattoos of pink butterflies. She was on the third lady when a ruckus broke out on the sidewalk outside the shop.

"Hey! You've gotta see this! It's Star Wars out here!" one of the waiting women shrieked.

Lily put down the tattoo machine and rushed to the window. There were seven people dressed head-to-toe in white Storm Trooper outfits doing a dance routine with a portable stereo. A crowd was gathering on the sidewalk.

The performers were carrying big black toy guns and making a huge racket shooting them and doing high kicks.

The tallest one stopped and yelled, "Lily this is for you! Your Snake LOVES you."

Lily wanted to disappear in embarrassment. The bridesmaids covered their mouths and giggled. Out on the streets a couple of news vans showed up. The local news channels were filming the gathering crowd and the Storm Trooper's antics. Taboo Tattoo was supposed to be edgy, dark and mysterious. A group of dancing cosplay Storm Troopers were not helping with that image. Her boss was going to be furious, and now it was on the news.

She tried to ghost Snake as he sent her text after text that week, ignoring every message. But he didn't give up, instead he showed up outside the shop in various costumes begging her to come over to his place for a Mario Cart marathon. One day he was a Power Ranger, the next The Green Lantern, the third time Deadpool. The week went by excruciating slow as she waited for Friday to arrive.

Finally, she took the streetcar to Pagan Possibilities in the wee hours of the morning and rushed into the garage as soon as the door was unlocked. If anything, there was more paraphernalia littering the occult store. Lavender incense was burning.

Penny sat behind the desk, a private little grin on her face. She had seen the dancing Storm Troopers on the news and heard the declarations of love and devotion. Once again, the magic ink had done its job.

"Penny, you have to reverse the power of the ink! Snake is not who I thought he was, this guy lives in his mom's basement and doesn't even have a job," Lily blurted.

"I told you to be sure before you imprinted him with it. You were warned," Penny said, ruffling the green ballroom gown she was wearing.

"I can't live with this. I don't want to spend my weekends playing fantasy games and travelling by bicycle. Plus, he's scaring off my customers! He shows up wearing cosplay costumes and it's really uncool."

"The special ink is much like regular tattoo ink; it will fade in time and so will its power. You'll just have to be patient. Snake will slowly lose his obsession with you."

"What do I do in the meantime?" Lily asked leaning over the desk, eyes wide in desperation.

"Join his Cosplay Club? Learn to love Dungeons and Dragons?" Penny chuckled.

# The Versa-Vice

~

First published: August 23, 2020
  Tales from the Dream Zone
  Flying Ketchup Press
  Genre: Speculative literary fiction
  Publisher/Editor: Polly McCann
  Pay: Contributor Copy x 2
  Previous rejections of The Versa Vice: 5

∾

Flying Ketchup Press

∾

Flying Ketchup Press is a family-owned independent press operating out of Kansas City. Polly McCann is the managing editor, and she says, "We think everything should be done with a sense of humor. When you work with us, it's like you are at our kitchen table."

McCann says, "Our idea is to help new and diverse voices in short story and poetry books. (We wanted a good satiable story that didn't involve 72 plus hours on the couch with *Netflix* or digging through old magazines at the library for cutting edge journals). We decided a small press could bring the two worlds together quickly and we decided to go old school— back to the day when a short story was a little longer, a bit more developed. It gets you noticed. Stories have a way of sticking with you, sometimes over a lifetime in a way that other genres don't. So, we set out to look for the next Hemingway, the next Washington Irving, the next Isaac Asimov, the next Ray Bradbury, the next Zora Neal Hurston, the next Flannery O'Connor, the next Shirley Jackson, and more. Plus, we want more women authors, more #weneeddiversebooks. We basically shook off an old idea and refilled it with a 21st-century mindset because we knew it was just the right size for us."

When asked what sort of stories FKP is looking for, she says, "Sci-Fi and fantasy short fiction is our main goal; short stories that take place in weird wild new worlds but it is the inner world that the story really addresses. The character's desires and decisions in facing their situations. However, we want to add some non-fiction collections to our shelf in the future. Is your story full of surprises, twists, mysterious creatures, technological wonder, and new things we've never thought of? Then welcome home to Flying Ketchup Press. Submit today!"

$\sim$

How "The Versa-Vice" found a home in *Tales from the Dream Zone*

$\sim$

"The Versa Vice" was the third fiction piece I ever wrote. I wanted to try the classic body swap story, and originally wrote it with two cis-gender girls, one beautiful, one plain. I submitted it to quite a few markets but just piled up form rejections. I needed to find a way to make my story stand out and many submission calls asked specifically for underrepresented characters. My very first story that made it to print was picked up by the LGBT issue of *The Gateway Review: A Journal of Magical Realism.* One of my characters was transgender in this odd futuristic short. (See the chapter on "Planet Nine.") I rewrote the characters in "The Versa Vice" and had one girl crushing on the other instead.

Flying Ketchup Press ran a contest on submittable.com asking for short stories dealing with the "dream theme." They wanted to create, "a collection of weird and wonderful stories that take place inspired by remembered or imagined dreams." I hit submit in October 2018 and in February 2019 got my acceptance. The actual publication of the book didn't happen until a year and a half later.

To date, this was the longest I've had to wait between a story getting accepted and seeing it in print. However, McCann kept in contact with her winners, assuring us the editing and production of the book was well underway. When they did get the ball rolling, the editors took a lot of time with my story, and I learned a lot in the process. They had me do an extensive rewrite, creating more of a character arc for both of my female protagonists. I asked McCann why she chose my tale:

"The Versa Vice is a great story. It has a nice contemporary feeling to it, but also adds a bit of that sci-fi with a post-modern edge. It's about a college freshman named Sherri who can't decide if she is in love with another classmate, Indira or if she is just a friend. After an incident, she thinks maybe they should be arch enemies. Sherri is a very real character who suffers from mistakes and low self-esteem as anyone in a new setting for the first time might. When she enters a psychology class experiment on dreams she finds she has a skill with lucid dreaming. It's interesting that Sherri's subconscious is filled with so many weak spots and insecurities. However, it is also the source of her strength; her gifts are actually superior to the other kids in the experiment. I think this is a great metaphor for all creatives. If we can access our inner creativity, if we can flip around a problem on its head, we will find our weaknesses are our strengths. That's what a lot of good stories are about. And Versa Vice has a great twist that way–as the name implies. (I won't give any more away.) There are many points you could debate, argue, and discuss in that one over dinner with friends. These stories are great for book clubs, classes, and just for fun."

There was no pay for this project, but I did receive two author copies. McCann wanted me to mention why they choose to give away author copies in lieu of payment,

"One thing about author copies is that you have a nice book you could sell at your events or readings. I hope that when we have more years under our belt and more sponsors, we can have monetary prizes and stipends for all our writers. We are building a traditional/ hybrid press from the ground up. Soon we hope to have a podcast and a few imprints etc. We are looking at ways to pay it forward especially with our poet in residence program."

~

Inspiration for "The Versa Vice"

~

When I was in university, we had to volunteer for experiments with the Psychology department to get our Psych 101 credit. I signed up for a study on susceptibility to hypnosis. It was a bizarre experience and I tried to recreate it in this short. Apparently, I was "highly susceptible". I always wondered if that could have led to something more sinister.

~

Lessons Learned

~

1) I WASN'T aware that Flying Ketchup Press never asked for first serial rights. It's a newbie error not to pay close attention to what you are, and are not, signing away. I was able to put "The Versa Vice" up for sale as a short story on Amazon while trying to teach myself the ropes of self-publishing because I still had all the rights.

2) Polly McCann is a wonderful contact and truly passionate about promoting her authors and books. She held a virtual author's reading and invited me to attend, and I somehow missed it. Never fail to embrace an opportunity to promote your work and meet other authors. I won't miss the next one.

~

REJECTIONS

~

CAST OF WONDERS

"Thank you for sending us "The Versa Vice". We appreciate the chance to read it. Unfortunately, the piece is not for us. Our readers felt the story was missing the developed sense of wonder or fantastic element that we consider the hallmark of Cast of Wonders stories. We didn't find the ending as unexpected as we would have liked, and thought some of the character tropes chosen were a little over-used. If you are still searching for a podcast or magazine to publish this story, you can find a list of recommend venues on our website under Markets. And say hello for us!"

.   .   .

Grindstone International Short Story Prize

"This is a very interesting piece in that the concept was unique and exciting. It's always fascinating to see where a piece ends up, especially when nothing is given away in the beginning. This is usually a good thing, but in your case, it's a little confusing because the genre of the story isn't immediately clear. It reads like a romantic comedy in the beginning, but ends up at science fiction/fantasy. This can throw off a reader, so while you've done a good job keeping the mystery intact and setting up the story, in a short piece like this, it's good to set the tone from the beginning too so the reader can get invested in the genre. The grammar and structure of the story needs to be worked on as well. There were constant tense shifts which were very distracting. Overall, the formatting needs a lot of work too. You should always start dialogue with a new line, and if you're switching from general narration to a character's inner monologue, you should use italics. If you're mentioning a TV show, use italics, and if you're already using italics for the rest of the text, then use regular font instead- either way, make sure it stands out from the rest of the text. I liked this story, but it needs a lot of work in order to bring it to publishable quality. You should take this as an opportunity to revisit the piece and edit it heavily. The concept is there, but if it isn't executed well, it just doesn't hold up on its own. Even the smallest grammatical error can throw the reader off, and as a writer, you want the reader to be so engrossed in the world you have created that they barely realize they're reading a story."

6

THE VERSA VICE

*W*as she in love with Indira? She was stunning with her lithe brown limbs, thick dark hair and eyes the colour of chocolate. Sherri thought she might be getting some reciprocal vibes from her. It was tough enough making friends, but trying to find that one special friend? Sherri hadn't come out to her parents -or even herself for that matter -until the final year of high school. Now here she was in her first year at university and she had never been kissed. By a boy or a girl.

Perhaps tonight her luck would change?

Indira, a classmate in her English Literature lectures, chatted with her about assignments and upcoming exams. Frequently those elegant hands would grab Sherri's arm or pat her on the knee.

It took her breath away. Girls like Indira never paid attention to Sherri; this was her high school fantasy come true. The popular girl wanted to be her friend! Maybe even more?

Yesterday with a lilting laugh and suggestive wink, her gorgeous companion suggested dinner. So far, the date had been going smashingly. They shared a vegan flatbread at Boston Pizza conversing about their classes. They were deep in the world of Joseph Conrad and his genius characterization. When they were done, Indira footed the bill and offered to drive her back home in her MINI Cooper. When she parked, Sherri leaned towards Indira with eyes closed, her lips pursed.

"Uhhh, Sherri I think you've got the wrong idea. I just needed help with my English Lit essay," Indira said leaning away from her with a frown.

Was it possible to roll out the car door and disappear into another dimension? Maybe Indira wasn't into girls, or just wasn't into Sherri. This was the most embarrassing moment of her life.

Was there another world where an alternate Sherri was living an amazing life? One whose brown hair was slightly less limp, eyes brighter blue, and physique more hourglass? At a minimum, she'd take better gay-dar.

"I've always had trouble with Joseph Conrad. For sure I will get a better mark now, well worth the price of a flatbread," Indira said.

As another dimension DID NOT open up and let Sherri slip out of existence, she put a big fake smile on her face.

"Right. Well thanks dinner. Keep your heart out of darkness."

Tears gathered at the corner of her eyes as she sat in the parking lot.

Did she really make a Joseph Conrad joke? Sherri grabbed her purse and stumbled out of the car walking in the other direction without looking back at Indira.

She should have known someone so stunning was out of

her league. It's only in movies like *Kissing Jessica Stein* where the hot girl starts a torrid affair.

Of course. When Indira took out her English Lit paper and asked about "civilized versus savage imagery"... Sherri should have known she was being used.

Sherri let the tears roll while trudging back up to her room. All that time carefully applying eye shadow, blush and mascara onto her pudgy pleasant face. She thought she looked halfway decent when she left the dorm, but now she was going to look like a Jackson Pollock painting. She crawled into bed. Maybe she would meet a cute girl in her dreams. Her eyes closed and she slipped into a deep sleep.

She's on the run and they're gaining on her. The terror. Her frantic search for help reveals no one on the empty street. Up ahead, there's the dull gleam of the subway entrance lights. A side street access, serviced by rotating cages and token machines.

She charges down the stairs almost slamming into the entrance barriers. A quick search of her pockets turns up lint, mints, but no token. She's trapped. Her two tormentors catch up with her. It's her vicious grade two teacher-- the one who used to whisper, "You are going to fail" in her ear. And her nasty high school Phys-Ed teacher who had singled her out in gym class calling her fat and unfit.

They advance on her...

She woke with a gasp. Pajamas sweat-soaked and heart pounding. She's had this dream before. After that nightmare, going back to sleep was unlikely. Sherri got dressed and went to find an early breakfast.

Avoiding the chilly September weather, she padded through the underground tunnels that connected all the buildings. There is a wall in the Student Center covered in post-its and flyers, one announcement read "Back-to-the-Books Bash! Phi Delta Theta Mixer for ALL university freshman. BYOB!"

Did she need to deliberately add more humiliating moments to her life this week? Who would she go with? Her eyes drifted down the board to another posting:

Looking for subjects for psychology experiment. Twenty dollars per participant. One hour. Friday September 22. 7:00pm. Psychology Lab B.

That was tonight! She ripped the posting off the wall and went in search of a chocolate chip muffin. High octane carbs would help fuel her for a day of classes. Luckily, there was no English Lit on Fridays. The day passed slowly. After a week of scribbling notes during lectures in theatres full of other first year students, she needed a break. Sherri wandered around until she found the campus pub. As long as she brought either a book or a laptop she could justify sitting at a table and not feel out of place.

There was an empty booth at the back. Sherri sat so she could people watch, then propped her laptop up in front of her. Foursomes were playing Euchre, study groups sat and talked, and couples flirted.

Indira. She was there holding court at the bar with three handsome guys hanging off her every word. Beautiful lips flashing and eyes glowing. She obviously loved the attention. That answered the gay question. Her laughter rung out over the bar. Sherri was too humiliated to go up and chat with her, and luckily her corner was dark enough to keep incognito.

One vodka and tonic later, Sherri went back to her room. She did not go to the fraternity mixer. Being a hamster in the experiment sounded better, actually. She quickly changed into clean yoga pants, a cotton sweater, coaxed her hair into a messy bun, and headed over to the Science building.

Psychology Lab B wasn't hard to find. It was There was the musty smell of body odour in the hallway- an industrial dingy grey made worse bu a few of the fluorescent tube lights flickering in the room. Quite a few people were waiting. Surprisingly, a lot of students were willing to spend their Friday night earning twenty dollars instead of partying.

Her stomach sank when the musical voice reached her ears. Indira was chatting with a nice looking fellow at the other side of the room. She flicked back her thick hair, caught Sherri's eye, and walked towards her.

"Sherri! How are you? Thanks for your help last night with my Conrad paper. I thought you spent most of your time studying. Glad to see you out and about," she looked down her nose.

"Sure, Indira. Whenever you need help let me know."

Could she be anymore of a door mat? It was time to find a quick exit; she didn't need twenty bucks that badly. Her stomach shuttered. Time to hightail it out of here. Wait. Her escape route suddenly blocked by a tall, thin man in a lab coat. Unkempt with grey hair, he sported a hipster beard, and his lab coat blended in with the tired grey of the walls.

"I'm Professor Ratcliff. We are conducting a study on the susceptibility of individuals for deep hypnosis. There are twenty of you registered here today, so we are going to do this in two groups of ten," he said, pacing in front of them. Consulting a clipboard, he read off the first ten names on his list.

Sherri heard her name called but not Indira's. She would stay if she didn't have to actually sit with the narcissistic mean girl.

"Would you all follow me into the lab," Ratcliff ordered, leading them forward.

The room featured a big round table set up with audio stations. The lighting was dim, with no exterior windows. The musty smell of sweaty bodies became stronger. Two assistants fluttered around, helping everyone find a seat. They put headphones on each student, and attached two probes to their temples. A soothing male voice came through her personal headphones with a British accent.

"This experiment will only last around half an hour, so get comfortable and focus on what I am saying. The sensors attached above your ears are going to be monitoring your brainwaves. You won't even notice them working. So please take a deep breath, close your eyes."

Sherri closed her eyes, took a deep breath, and let the melodious voice wash over her.

"Let's start by taking notice of how our bodies are feeling today. Starting with the top of our heads and working down to our feet, assess how each body part is feeling. Imagine a warm ray of sunshine flowing into the top of your head and start to travel down through your body. Bringing warmth, bringing comfort, and making you feel very sleepy..."

With a start, Sherri jerked up from her chair when she felt a set of hands on her shoulders. She hadn't even noticed that she'd fallen asleep.

"You missed your cue to come out of the hypnosis," the assistant said. "I bet we are going to find you highly susceptible."

Sherri stood up and followed the rest of the group to collect her cash on the way out the door. Should she go to the pub to do more people watching? No, she didn't want to bump into Indira there, so instead went back to her dorm room to turn in for the night.

Monday morning, a text came in from an unknown number.

"Please return to the Psych Lab B Monday evening (tonight) at 6:00 pm. We have some follow up from Friday's experiment. Please text C to confirm. You will receive another $20 payment."

"C" Sherri texted back. Why were they being called back?   During classes that day, she found it very hard to concentrate.

She stood outside the door of Psych Lab B at exactly 6:00 pm, but instead of throngs of milling students, this time she was the only one. Then she heard some footsteps hurrying down the hall. Lightfast heels tapping.

It was Indira, her cheeks flushed as she stopped beside Sherri. Of course, little miss perfect was also going to be here. It was just her luck. Why did she have to be so gorgeous? Sherri's stomach roiled and clenched.

"Hi! Are we the only ones here? I wonder what this is about?" Indira asked, one hand on a taunt hip.

How could Indira act like that awkward moment in her Mini Cooper never happened? It was like she had no empathy whatsoever. She was trying to think of something witty to say when the Professor opened the door with a manic look on his face.

"I'm so glad the both of you made it! Come on in! We have lots and lots of work to do. So much work..." he said his whole body agitating vertically.

The girls exchanged confused looks and followed him in. The two assistants were there again. Instead of looking bored, they both smiled. Eyes bright like it was Christmas morning.

"What we were doing at the last experiment was searching for people susceptible to hypnosis, ...able to be deeply hypnotized. But we are also looking for something else. Something far more exciting. We are looking for students who can potentially lucid dream. And you two, you were off the charts! It's luckily to find one student a year who MAY be able to accomplish the higher levels of lucid dreaming. But to find two of you in one session! And such strong markers!" Ratcliff paced back and forth in front of them.

"Umm. Lucid dreaming? What's that?" Indira asked.

"Lucid dreaming is when you are aware you are dreaming and can control what is happening in your dream. Having control over the subconscious sleeping mind may be the key to unlocking the hidden abilities of the human brain," Ratcliff said rubbing his hands together.

"What if I'm not interested in participating in this?" Most of Sherri's dreams were nightmares. She's not sure she wanted to spend any extra time in that creepy dreamland. Plus, how much being close to Indira could she take? She couldn't forget the embarrassment of their previous encounter.

Panic flashed over Ratcliff's face, "you will be handsomely rewarded for your time! And it won't take up much of it. No, not much of it at all! I can even see about maybe granting you extra credit for being involved. Sherri, your markers are the highest I have ever seen. "

"Well, hard to turn down extra credit," Sherri said. It was nice to be recognized as good at something, even if she didn't quite understand what. Maybe she can learn to dream about rainbows and waterfalls instead of vengeful teachers?

"With two of you," Ratcliffe said, "we can take our research even further. This project has been going on for three years. Past participants are controlling their dreams and have full recall when they awake. However, we haven't been able to achieve interaction. Both of you demonstrate a remarkably high amount of beta-1 frequency in your brains. And the amount of activity in your parietal lobes is off-the-charts. We are hoping that the two of you can meet in the dream state, control your interactions within the dreams, and interact with each other."

Sherri tries not to frown.

"Imagine the implications," Ratcliffe continued. "Espionage, military uses..."

Military uses? Spy stuff? Sherri didn't like the implications, but Indira didn't look worried. "Cool. Money and extra credit? I'm in."

"I'm in too," Sherri said. It could help fund the college research department, how could she quit now?

"Okay, let's get this going. I've had so many failures with other students, but with you two..." Professor Ratcliff said with a big smile cracking his wrinkled face. "Follow me! Yes, into our inner sanctum."

He led them out of the waiting area, past all the headphone stations and into a room with two retrofitted dental office chairs. One wall was all glass with monitoring devices. Rows of desks perched on the other side. Through another set of doors, the two girls and assistants followed the scientist with a spring in his step.

"Okay let's get you set up here! Sherri you are here in this chair and, Indira, in the other, please," Ratcliff gestured to the scary-looking recliners. At least the air seemed fresher in here with a new coat of paint on the walls.

The two assistants set up the girls with temple probes and added extra monitors to their arms, legs, chest, back and belly areas. Sherri whispered, "I feel like Frankenstein's wife. If they bring out anal probes, I'm jetting. "

The assistant had "Chan" on a little card pinned to his shirt. "The extra probes are for recording your isometric muscle movements. We are hoping to understand and document all your emotions in the dream state. It will be interesting to see if you and Indira can actually interact with each other and we can see if your motions are corresponding with these machines." He slipped the headphones onto Sherri's ears.

The other assistant, a small thin woman named Heather, hooked up Indira. Then the doctors left the enclosed room.

The headphones filled with the soothing British voice, "you are feeling very sleepy. Very very sleepy. Concentrate on your breathing. Feel the breath slowly fill your body and then gently exhale. Let's think about the beach. A white sandy beach with little rocks that roll beneath your bare feet as you walk the sand... the endless sand. Look out on the water as the waves lap and lap and lap. It's endless, it's soothing... listen to the waves..."

A white sandy beach with lapping waves sparkles in front of distant cliffs. Scrub grass grows on the dunes beside her. Soon, very far off, she sees another figure strolling on the beach. At first, an unrecognizable silhouette, Sherri decides to close the distance between them. She runs, kicking up the dirt beneath her bare feet. She loves the roughness of the grains of sand, scraping her heels, and squelching through her toes. It feels so real. Somehow she knows it's a dream. Wait. Normal rules don't apply here. Right? Sherri concentrates on her legs. They move faster.

Now she's flying, almost running on top of the beach, no

longer having her feet sink into the damp sand. The wind is in her hair. Freedom.

Wait. It's Indira. Sherri digs her heels into the sand, tumbles into the surf, and the cold water drenches her.

Indira jumps back with a big grin to avoid getting splashed.

"It works! We are both in the same dream. Sherri, I would have said this is impossible but look at us! Together."

Sherri pulls herself up off the ground, shaking white foam and sand out of her hair. "So. Let's have some fun."

What's that? A few feet offshore, an enormous dragon pushes up through the waves. It soars over the girls. They both duck and get drenched in the waterfall cascading off its body.

"Lookout," Sherri calls.

"What was that!?" Indira yells over the splash and fiery roar.

"I made it! I imagined it," says Sherri. "Try it. Your turn!"

Indira crinkles up her nose and stares towards the horizon. A horse with a big horn sprouting out of its forehead gallops down the beach. The body is opaque, but the ocean glimmers through it. Rather than a frothy pounding of hooves, there's just the sound of the waves. When it gets closer, it dissolves and merges with the foam.

"Wow. That's harder than it looks," Indira gasps hugging her knees to stop the dizziness.

Finally, something Sherri does that outshines this girl who is perfect at everything. The sky gets darker, blurry and then fades away.

"You are now going to wake up, feeling refreshed and ready to go on with your day," a melodious voice instructs them from the air.

Sherri opened her eyes and had to blink a few times before the blurry lab became clear. A smile tickled her lips like a cat who just lapped up a bowl of cream.

Indira also woke up, panicking, and trying to rip her headphones off but gets tangled in some cords. Heather rushed in to help her.

"It worked. OMG, I think it worked. At first, it didn't seem like you were interacting at all with each other, but then your movements were totally coordinated. I wish we could have kept you under longer! But slowly to start, we mustn't exhaust you."

"What was going on with you at the end, Sherri?" Chan asked. "I thought for a moment you were in trouble, and I wanted to pull the plug and bring you out immediately, but Dr. Ratcliffe said to keep you under. That you were producing endorphins of pleasure not of stress. I've never seen a student pick this up so quickly."

As they walked out of the pod, Dr. Ratcliff beamed and was practically dancing on the spot.

Sherri smiled at him but said nothing. She needed to do some careful thinking about this. Where Indira looked flustered, Sherri was calm.

"Well, I think we have something here. We actually have something. Just when I thought the funding was drying up. Chen, you take Sherri and record everything she can remember about her time in the lucid state, and Heather you do the same with Indira," Ratcliff said, eyes glinting with glee.

After their debriefings, Indira invited Sherri to go to the pub.

"You have to tell me about those Wonder Woman moves of yours!" Indira asked, "How did you run so fast? And your dragon kicked my unicorn's butt. You are pretty great Sherri, an English Lit genius and now a superstar Lucid Dreamer," Indira pushed a strand of Sherri's hair behind her ear.

Was she flirting? Or did she not know how her touch put Sherri's system into red alert?

"Sorry, maybe next time. I'm crazily exhausted after all that lucid dreaming stuff. Time for some normal sleep," Sherri said heading quickly down the hall.

She might be a dragon-conjuring wonder woman in her dream state, but now she was just fat Sherri. The Sherri who'd never even been kissed. She slipped on her fuzzy pajamas and curled under the sheets.

That night Sherri had another dream:

She's running. Running for her life as the blood courses through her and panic fuels every step. Her teachers are after her again. Then she stops. She turns to wait.

They materialize out of the darkness looking like characters from the Mad Max remake.

Sherri says, "stop. I command you," a great booming noise comes out instead of her usual soft voice. She sounds like The Wizard from Oz.

They do stop. Expressions of confusion replacing their usual teachers-from-hell countenances.

"Why are you chasing me?" she asks.

Her grade two teacher's face contorts into an ugly snarl. "Because you are stupid. And you are going to fail fail fail. You will never be smart enough for grade three."

Sherri snorts, "I passed grade three a long time ago. I'm not stupid. Go away and don't come back."

Then she looks up at the sky and her enormous dragon drops down with a yowl and snatches up the elementary school teacher. Sherri can hear the screaming as the bony old woman is carried away into the night.

The Phys-Ed teacher steps forward like a Pokémon gearing up for his battle turn, "You can never make a team. You are too slow. Too fat."

Sherri doesn't even bother arguing with him. She looks down at the ground and a big hole of water opens up beneath the sneering man. He drops with a splash and a hoard of very hungry fish with sharp teeth attack him. Sherri watches him thrash until he's dragged under, leaving only a bloody pool. Then the pool disappears and the street lamps come back on. It is an ordinary street in an ordinary neighbourhood with nothing frightening about it at all.

Waking up, Sherri feels like a new woman. No stomach issues. More powerful. More capable. And she had an idea... a delightfully devilish idea. It rolled around in her subconscious, growing like a well-watered seed, slowly taking root.

At the next scheduled lucid dreaming session, Sherri walked with an extra lilt in her step. She met Indira in the hall,

"Hi! Enjoying the experiment?" Sherri let her eyes roam over Indira's lithe curves.

"I always knew I was meant to do something big. This is groundbreaking research and you are going to help me be as good at it as you are, aren't you Sherri?" purred Indira as they waited outside the lab door.

"Maybe I can teach you my techniques after hours. So, you are in what dorm?" asked Sherri, she needed to know where Indira lived for her plan to work.

"I am in the co-ed dorm, edge of campus."

"What room number?" Sherri asked, giving Indira's firm bicep a light squeeze.

"Three-oh-two. Of course I have one of the few single

rooms given to first-year students," Indira said flexing a little under Sherri's grasp.

"The co-ed building. 302. Got it," Sherri grinned.

The door opened and Professor Ratcliff ushered them in. If possible, he radiated with even more energy than the last time.

"I can't wait to hear what you dream next. The Beta activity! The monitors! I've never seen anything like it! Sherri are you sure you haven't done this before? Yes, what will you dream next?" He jittered on the spot.

The girls went straight to their chairs to be strapped in by Chen and Heather. The room dimmed and the girls are hypnotized back to the dream world on the beach.

The familiar feel of sand is between her toes, and she can feel the cool ocean breeze. She sees Indira further down the beach again. She runs right at her, picking up as much speed as she can.

The faster she goes, the higher the waves crash aggressively onshore. A chilly wind whips Indira's thick black hair around her face.

Indira smiles when she sees Sherri getting closer, but then her expression turns to concern.

"Slow down Sherri, you're running too fast. You're going to..."

CRASH. Sherri pummels into Indira. She doesn't slow down even a fraction. The collision between their bodies creates a searing pain.

Sherri woke up with a gasp and the worst headache ever. She kept her eyes closed for a minute as she waited for the intensity of the throbbing to subside. When she does open her eyes, she felt long hair tickling the sides of her face. Running her hands down her waist, she doesn't find soft fat flesh. Instead, there was a flat belly. Her hands slid up to her chest and felt two large lovely mounds. Much bigger and firmer than her own.

A big smile crossed her face. She could get used to this perfect body. Now she knows, she didn't love Indira. She wanted to BE Indira.

She's done with Professor Ratcliff's experiment.

"Can someone please come unstrap me? I have places to go." It's not going to be hard to get that first kiss now, she smirked.

From the chair beside her came a loud terrified scream.

7

SOTEIRA PRESS

he Rougarou

FIRST PUBLISHED: December 13, 2019
The Monsters We Forgot V.3
Soteira Press
Genre: Horror
Editors: Gabriel Grobler & Rachele Bowman
Pay: Royalties $46.39 US to date.
Previous rejections of The Rougarou: 9

∾

Soteira Press

∾

SOTEIRA PRESS IS an indie publisher predominately interested in horror and the macabre. They publish a series of regional American horror anthologies called Horror USA. Some of their titles include *Horror USA: California, Horror USA: Texas, Horror USA: Washington*. This series is filled with horror stories full of "darkest, scariest, weirdest, most terrifying elements" each state has to offer. In addition to *The Monsters We Forgot*, they have anthology series out and upcoming called *What Monsters Do for Love, Monsters of the Water, Monsters of the Earth*, and *Monsters of the Air, Monsters of Fire, Monsters of the Void*, and *The Monsters We Become.*

Rachele Bowman says, "in the nearish future we'll be opening up to single-author titles."

∾

HOW "THE ROUGAROU" found a home in *The Monsters We Forgot*

∾

THIS WAS the first market I sent a story to that listed "royalties" as payment. It did put some money into my PayPal account. I received two payments from Rachele Bowman for $19.76 and $26.63 "Royalties for 'The Monsters We Forgot'". This series found some success on Amazon. A Facebook post on the Soteira Press page says, "Congratulations to the authors of "The Monsters We Forgot" - you've cracked the top 200 of the ENTIRE Kindle store!"

It took me a while to place this story, but I rewrote it every time I got a rejection. Unfortunately, none of the editors originally gave me any feedback, which is discouraging, but the norm for the industry. Editors sometimes get hundreds of submissions. Instead of giving up, I asked family members and friends to read "The Rougarou" and review it critically. Sometimes those closest to you try and spare your feelings and don't make the best editors. However, my mother found some plot holes, my sister let me know what parts were "too gross", and my best friend suggested more description. With each suggestion, I reworked the story and found a new place to submit it to. My favorite resource is horrortree.com, which lists current calls for submissions for short stories, novellas, and even novels. I also found some on ralan.com, and publishedtodeath.blogspot.com.

I submitted "The Rougarou" to four magazines, three anthologies and two podcasts. All rejected it. But as the story got better, my rejections started to get more personalized. I rewrote the story until it finally got picked up by Soteira Press. The editing process with Gabriel Grobler and Rachele Bowman was painless, as they did the work themselves and then sent me an email, "Attached, please find your story for *The Monsters We Forgot* as it will appear in the published anthology. If you have any corrections, questions, or objections, please let me know as soon as possible."

I was happy with the edits and was excited to read the anthology. My contract with them did not include author copies, so I bought two for a total of $25.29. Which of course cuts my profit from this story ($46.39) more than in half.

～

The Inspiration

～

My brother and his wife decided they were sick of city life in Toronto and bought a little house in the middle of nowhere in northern Ontario. Literally in the middle of nowhere. The closest store was an hour away. They were surrounded by trees, mosquitos, and a few odd neighbours. The thick bush was perfect cover for creatures of the imagination.

～

Lessons Learned

～

1) If you want to make a net gain from your writing, beware of how many author copies you purchase. Unless you are sales motivated and are able to resell the ones you buy (keeping one for yourself of course), it's another way to empty your pocket book.

～

Rejections

～

"THANK you for submitting your story "The Rougarou". We regret to inform you we will not be accepting your submission for our Creatures theme. To give you a bit of feedback, we didn't find your story very well organized.

And a quick side note: I own draft horses myself, so I understand the hard work that goes into horse logging! What a fascinating job! I hope you will be able to find a home for your with another publisher. Good luck in your future writing endeavors."

8

THE ROUGAROU

My husband Benoit was moving the two of us up north, where the summers are short and the winter creates frostbite patches on your skin. Being originally from Louisiana, my Creole blood didn't like the cold. This was Canadian logging country, in one of the least inhabited areas of Ontario. Grocery shopping was a day trip, and the closest neighbour was an hour's snowmobile ride away.

Our romance started at a big television network in Toronto. I sold commercial airtime and Benoit was the creative lead in the marketing department. More than just our ad campaigns clicked. I was instantly attracted to this burly man with an amazing imagination. We also connected through our French Louisiana roots. His ancestors were run out of Nova Scotia and settled there before migrating back to Quebec, and my descendants came from African slaves brought to work on French colonial plantations. We both loved reading the history and colourful superstitions of our New Orleans culture. We made an odd couple, my petit frame and coffee-coloured skin next to his hulking body and red-headed paleness. He proposed to me by piercing an arrow through a voodoo doll's heart with a ring attached to it.

There was great content on Netflix that featured legends of our people, including some spine-tingling horror movies. Unfortunately, we weren't the only ones who loved Netflix. As more and more TV viewers cut the cord and cancelled their cable subscriptions, conventional television suffered. We were both let go when the company's shares sank to penny stock level. The owners filed for bankruptcy protection, and hundreds of people were walked out the door without severance packages.

My husband had an odd weekend hobby where he liked to drive into the Canadian Shield forests and strap chains to Belgian horses (Belgians are the strongest breed of heavy horse) and skid logs out of forests. Wealthy land owners found it a novelty to hire him for a weekend. It put a few dollars in his pockets and kept him in incredible shape. Environmental horse logging was a dying art but his grandfather had cleared land with draft horses for a living up in the Gatineau region of Quebec, so Ben came by it naturally. When his grandfather died, Ben took the two old horses and boarded them at a stable north of Toronto with big grassy fields. He said working with Betty and Bob the Belgians reminded him of his Acadian roots.

We'd put off starting a family to focus on our careers and now neither of us had one. Toronto was an expensive city, and regular jobs in short supply so I couldn't say no when he found a lucrative job as a logger almost four hours northeast. He was hired to clear trees near Bon Echo Park for a rich family who wanted to open a private campground.

Using horses to do the logging made sense to keep the trails and land undamaged.

Part of Benoit's pay was free furnished accommodation on a small acreage with a barn for Betty and Bob, his grandfather's Belgians. We were renting a condo in downtown Toronto, so we broke the lease and sold all our furniture on Kijiji. If I thought that process made me miserable, I had no idea what was in store for me. We packed up his pickup truck with the bare essentials, our large American Bulldog Daisy, and started the long drive north.

I'd thought cottage country was the wilderness. Wrong. Once we got into the County of Frontenac, it was obvious why no one had settled here after the early logging boom. The land was hilly, harsh and truly remote. For the last hour there wasn't a restaurant, store, or even a poutine stand, only a few old lonely shacks here and there.

After what seemed forever, Ben pulled into a two-acre property with an old double-wide trailer on blocks. It backed onto a huge forest so it would be easy for him to hitch up the horses and get to work. But I couldn't see anything else good about it. The house had aluminum siding, a crooked porch, and small windows. Smoke billowed out of the chimney and a pile of logs sat outside. Great. Probably no central heating.

"Ben, you've got to be kidding?" I asked as we turned onto the snow-covered property.

"Hey, it's not that bad! It's only for a year Louisa. Think how much fun you are going to have keeping the fireplace stocked with wood," he gave me a big grin and reached over Daisy's back to give my short black hair a ruffle.

I kept my mouth shut. There was really nothing he could do about it. And I loved him, so I was going to endure this. We unpacked and settled the horses into the small barn. At least the stables were quaint with an old-school hay loft and a wide aisle down the middle. Going back into the trailer-house I turned the tap at the cracked ceramic sink to get a glass of water. It was an odd yellow colour and smelled like sulphur. Good thing we had some bottled water. There wasn't a fireplace, but instead a black wood stove that ate logs voraciously. Mysterious stains marked the walls.

I could get used to the rundown furnishings, well water, and wood stove. What I couldn't get used to was the howling. Every night the eerie serenade of a wolf made my blood run cold.

"Ben, do you hear that?" I asked shaking him awake the first few nights after he crawled into bed exhausted from logging.

"It's just the January winds. They pick up coming down the mountain side," he said giving me a hug and promptly falling back asleep.

Labouring all day in the freezing cold made him sleep like the dead. Benoit got up with the sun and took Betty and Bob out to pull down oak and ash trees. He didn't return till sundown. Then he had to bed down the horses and give them grain and fresh water before coming in himself.

There is nothing quite like the smell of man sweat mixed with horse, manure, and chainsaw oil. Ben would take off his wet boots and hang the insoles by the fire along with his damp pants and jacket. The whole house would be permeated with the foul odour. One more thing I had to learn to tolerate. I didn't sleep well at night and it made me edgy. I was sure the howling was intensifying. That was not the wind. I took comfort from Daisy's big warm body draped over my feet. I'm sure my 140lb bulldog could take on a supersized wolf. Or at least distract it while I ran away.

After about a week of huddling in the house, trying to make it homey, it was time to brave the cold. I hadn't ventured into thigh-high snow yet, but by now Ben and his skidding equipment had made a good trail. Shivering with teeth chattering, I got out of bed and bundled up with sweat pants and three sweaters. There was coffee left in the bottom of the pot, so I poured myself a cup of the now thick sludge and pulled on my boots, snow pants and thick down jacket. The puffy coat along with three sweaters made a scarf redundant. I could hardly turn my neck already doing my impersonation of the Stay Puft Marshmallow Man.

Daisy and I headed out the backdoor and started following Ben's footprints to the barn. The real path would start there. The cold made my nostril hairs freeze and my lungs started a long slow burn. When I got to the barn, I pulled open the sliding door and went in to warm up for a minute. The horses truly lived in nicer digs then we did. Climbing the wood rung ladder, I went up to explore the hay loft. There were spiderwebs coating the window at the end. Rubbing a hole in the dirt, I peered out at endless miles of trees up the mountain. A gorgeous sight with the sun reflecting off the tips of the Fir and Pine trees. I made a plan to get cross-country skis next time we went to town.

Looking down to the side I saw a big indentation in the hay, like something has been laying there. Bending down for a closer look I saw some rough black and brown hair. Bear, maybe? Picking up a clump, the coarse mass certainly wasn't bear. The thought that it might be the wolf I heard howling made me shiver even in the warm barn under my layers. I noticed the hay still felt warm. Getting up quickly I hustled back to the ladder. Just before my head dropped past the loft floor, I saw two masked black eyes staring at me. An enormous raccoon strolled out from behind a round bale and settled back in her spot. I felt a little ridiculous, what kind of monster was I imagining anyways? Daisy was in the aisle waiting for me. We headed out of the barn, but my unfounded fear had coated me in sweat and I didn't want to catch a worse chill. I abandoned the winter walk idea and decided to tell Ben that we had a raccoon issue when he got home. The creature was probably stealing all our horse grain.

Except he did not come home that evening. Our spicy seafood stew sat untouched in the slow cooker.

Daisy and I waited by the backdoor staring down the trail as the sun sank behind the mountain. I tried to will the sight of the old Belgians and Ben to appear, but nothing happened. Cold terror crept up the back of my spine.

Rather than sit still and let the very last rays of light disappear, I put on all my warm gear again and grabbed an industrial-sized flashlight. This time Daisy and I rushed all the way down the footpath, past the barn, and onto the horses' skidding trail. As soon as we entered the forest, the little bit of light from the sun was obscured. It was really dark. I couldn't tell if the icy chill I was feeling was from the cold or from dread. Walking as fast as I could on the icy trail, I tried not to look into the black trees on either side of me. Daisy scampered eagerly through the undergrowth, her nose guiding her. This was her first real walk off the property.

"Benoit! Are you out here! Ben! Call out if you need help!" I hollered every few feet.

At first, I heard nothing back, but then a long slow howl filled the air. I stopped in my tracks and my heart thudded to an awful full stop. Daisy nudged me and a low growl emanated from her throat. Piercing the night, I heard the eerie howl again and my feet moved me forward before I became paralyzed with fear. Rushing forward into the black, only the thin light from the flashlight stopped me from tripping over roots.

Up ahead I could see a clearing made by Ben's logging efforts. Charging into the wide-open space, a glow came from the full moon cresting over the trees. Once again, I heard the howl. A big chestnut horse burst out of the trees on the far side and came galloping across the clearing. By the white stripe on her face I could tell it was Betty. She had her hauling collar on but was missing the rest of the harness and chains. She came straight for me but luckily, she slid to a stop before trampling me and I raised a hand to her cheek. Her eyes were wide open with the whites of them showing and sweat coated her body. A froth covered her chest and neck.

"Whoa girl. Where's Benoit?" Where's your partner Bob?" I said as I stroked her neck calmingly.

My eyes quickly assessed her body and I noticed a bit of blood on her side. Uh oh. Before I could take a closer look, the howl started up again, and this time it sounded very close. Betty reared up and galloped down the path towards home.

Now I knew something terrible had happened. Was the team attacked by a wolf pack? Where was Benoit? He would never leave his horses. Up ahead I saw a dark form laying in the snow by the edge of the clearing. Daisy charged ahead of me and started whining with joy. It must be Ben. Running at full tilt, I crashed onto the snow beside him and pushed Daisy back from licking his face.

"It's me, Louisa, are you okay?"

His eyes were open and he stared silently at me.

"What happened? Are you hurt?" I asked while scanning his body for injury.

I couldn't see anything immediately wrong with him until he pointed at his leg. His chainsaw pants were ripped and I could see blood underneath them.

"Did you cut your leg with your chainsaw? Can you walk?" I gasped, trying to get the dwindling glow from the flashlight close enough so I could take a better look.

"I... I didn't cut my leg. I was bitten."

"What? Bitten by what?" I said, trying to fight tears, but keeping my panic under control. I was going to have to get us out of here.

Just then the low howl started up again, and Daisy turned and took off into the trees.

"Daisy! No, Daisy come back!" I screamed into the darkness.

"Let her go Louisa and help me up," Ben grabbed my arm. I tried to get his massive frame off the ground. After a few minutes of slipping and grunting it worked and we were both standing.

"Where is Bob?" I asked as we slowly start walking towards home. He's limping and leaning heavily on me. "I saw Betty on the way here."

"I'm sorry honey, but Bob is gone." He said, deep sadness choking his voice.

"Gone? How?" I clung to his arm and focused on putting one step in front of the other.

"He was also bitten by this thing... when I tried to defend him, it gave me a bite. Then dragged him away, chains, harness and all. Betty shook free and took off," his French accent strong, as it always was when he became emotional.

"Bitten by what? A wolf?" I said looking down at his

bloody leg. It seems to have clotted up, thank goodness an artery wasn't hit.

"No. Not a wolf. Did your grandmother in New Orleans tell you tales of a man with a wolf's head? The Rougarou? Mon dieu," he said.

"Yes, if I didn't go to church, she told me the Rougarou would come for me. Every kid in my neighbourhood was terrified into good behaviour with stories about the legendary monster. So. You are trying to tell me you were bit by what. A Cajun werewolf?" I asked in disbelief.

As if to accent my question, the howling started up again. I heard the rapid pounding of paws behind us, but as I turned ready to fight, I saw it was just Daisy. Thank goodness.

We were almost home and Benoit was picking up the pace, "Louisa, I'm not imagining anything. It had a human body with long claws on its hands and a wolf's head."

I didn't respond immediately, but tried to remember the story my grandmother told me, always trying to frighten me into going to those long boring Catholic services. Some part of the story was niggling at my brain.

We were at the barn now and Betty was waiting at the door. I leaned Benoit against the side wall to let her into the barn and her stall. Luckily her heated bucket was already filled with water, so I just tossed some hay at her. She calmed down as soon as she started munching. But her eyes flicked in confusion at the empty stall beside her.

Grabbing a hold of Benoit again, we staggered into our house and I set him down on the couch. He pulled off his chainsaw pants and snow gear while I got some warm water, iodine and bandages. It did look like a creature had taken a chunk out of his leg. After cleaning it up and disinfecting it, I dressed him in his flannel pjs and gave him a glass of scotch. I rarely drink but I got one for myself as well.

I remember my grandmother's story clearer now. The heat of the whiskey cleared my mind and boiled in my mouth.

"Do you remember the rest of the legend Benoit? The part about how the Rougarou is under the spell for 101 days? Then after drawing human blood the curse is transferred to his victim?" I took a big gulp of my scotch and looked at him.

His eyes grew wide. He remembered. A new shiver rippled through me.

9

PULP MODERN

A Time to Forget

〜

First published: November, 2019
Pulp Modern: Tech Noir Special
Pulp Modern
Genre: Science Fiction
Publisher/Editor: Alec Cizak
Pay: $15
Previous rejections of A Time to Forget: 3

~

Pulp Modern

~

"NO SUBJECT IS TABOO," the submission guidelines state. Alec Cizak is the man behind the magazine and he says "I started publishing Pulp Modern because I didn't see any journals at the time that brought the major genres together. I also didn't see any big-time publications publishing riskier stories, so I felt there was a need for a market that could take chances since no advertising dollars were on the line. That's not a slam on the majors, by the way. I understand they are beholden to advertisers who may not want to be associated with gut-honest stories about junkies, pimps, and hookers."

Pulp Modern publishes crime, fantasy, science fiction, horror and westerns. In the *Pulp Modern: Tech Noir Special*, the art is captivating and provocative.

The world of pulp speculative fiction is its own microcosm. I love the community of writers involved in creating and supporting it. I follow Alec Cizak and many of the authors co-published with me in this issue on Twitter. In my opinion, the most entertaining tweeters out there.

The question most of us writers have (of course) is "where is the money?" I made $15, but then spent $18.25 ordering three author copies. Is the publisher recouping much? I asked Cizak if there was any profit margin.

"Nope. This is, financially, a losing venture. The recent Tech Noir issue cost about six hundred dollars to produce. It's generated about fifty dollars in sales and I doubt that number will even double. This is a labor of love. The independent pulp fiction community has had lags over the last ten years or so, moments where there were almost no markets for new writers, and I've gone through periods where I thought I would quit, but enough people would write to me and insist I keep Pulp Modern going that I gave in every time and got back to it. There are many, many writers out there. Some of them are really good and they don't have connections in the publishing world. A journal like Pulp Modern is there to make sure those unheard voices are heard."

How "A Time To Forget" found a home in *Pulp Modern: Tech Noir*

I HAD no idea this sub-genre of fiction existed when I started submitting my stories to every open call I could find. There are a few "sexbots" and "anti-heroes" in this issue full of dark futuristic musings. I never envisioned my work as "pulp" but love the way my story fits in with all the other dystopian shorts. I didn't even send my story to this magazine, instead I responded to a submission call for Switchblade Magazine, and my acceptance read:

"This is an intriguing, multi-POV piece, from a strong female perspective. It would be perfect for The Sun, if they were doing a Future-themed issue. It isn't what we normally do. But still, we like it. It provides great juxtaposition to our more, well, testosterone-driven pieces. We received a great deal of strong submissions for our Tech Noir themed issue. So many, that we reached out to some associates of ours, Pulp Modern, about doing a companion issue. We (Alec Cizak, Managing Editor for Pulp Modern, and I) decided to build and release two Tech Noir issues: *Switchblade: Tech Noir*, and *Pulp Modern: Tech Noir*. Both will be released at the same time (targeted release date October 2019). Pulp Modern (if you're not familiar with it) is a similar indie pulp magazine that has been around 5 years longer than Switchblade and has a slightly wider readership. If the story is still available, we'd like to publish it in *Pulp Modern: Tech Noir*.

Sincerely,

Scotch Rutherford"

Alec was a tough editor and gave me a good lesson about keeping my tenses correct. (Something I still struggle with.) The stories by the other authors in this issue really grabbed me, I found the tales to be edgy, sexy, well-crafted, and each has a quick punch at the end. The art in the *Pulp Modern: Tech Noir* is provocative and as interesting as the stories themselves.

Inspiration for "A Time to Forget"

Who isn't afraid of a future where we have no privacy? Every detail of our lives is on social media. Data mining is rampant. Corporations are thriving and growing larger as small businesses are forced to close their doors. Plus, why are so many people suffering from dementia? I took some of my futuristic fears and the result was "A Time to Forget".

Lessons Learned

1) Submission calls can be fluid. I submitted to Switchblade, but had my story published in Modern Pulp.

2) Twitter is a good tool. Many of the authors in this anthology, including the editor Alec Cizak are active on Twitter. I did a writing retreat with Heather O'Neill (Canadian novelist) and she recommended Twitter as the best way to connect with authors, agents, and publishers. After reading each story in the Tech Noir issue, I wrote a little review about it and tagged the author and Cizak. Pulp writers are a fascinating bunch and it was great to connect with them. #angeliquereviews

Rejections

I thought the world was interesting and the story was well-written, but while it was a straightforward projection from current trends, it was too much of a straight line projection, without the twists and turns that you usually find in real history. For example, no matter how luxurious a society is, there are always people who opt out.

Also, I found the idea of cellphones causing cancer in people's heads less believable than it would have been in the early 2000s. While modern smartphones are heavily used, they don't spend much time near people's heads, and they usually come with headsets."

10
———

A TIME TO FORGET

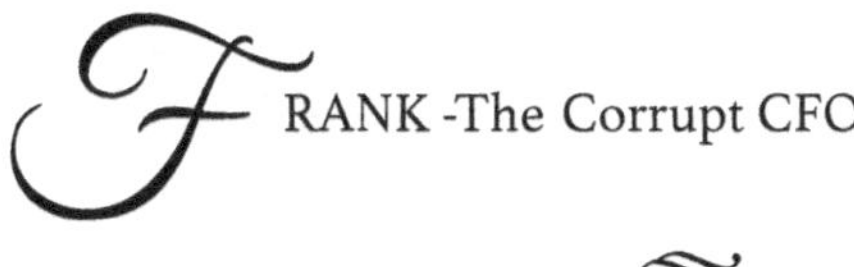
RANK -The Corrupt CFO

FRANK LOOKED over the stunning vista of the Connected Colonies capital city while standing on the roof of his condo building. It was a premium address for those with top social credits and high income right by the lake. The sun was coming up and the ripples of the water looked like a magical dance floor of twinkling fairies. Since when did he wax so poetic? He was a numbers guy. He put his hand to his head and bumped it a few times. His memory was failing him. When he tried to recall simple things, like what he ate for lunch, there was... nothing. Renegade websites created buzz about the link between new cellphone technology and Alzheimer's, but people loved their devices. Besides, there was no proof right? The Corp made sure of that.

He closed his eyes, took a deep breath and enjoyed the crisp tang of the air. The city was clean and quiet at this time of the day. Perhaps thirty years ago there would have been garbage blown into gutters, drunks "sleeping it off" on park benches and a few heroin-addicted hookers cashing in on the early morning trade. Thanks to The Corp and its authoritarian methods mixed with socialism and a social credit system, many of the old problems were abolished or at least controlled. I used to be so proud of being the CFO of The Corp. How could I have been so stupid?

He had been researching tech history for a town hall company meeting when he found the top secret documents. They detailed buried research on cognitive issues being linked to mobile devices. He downloaded the files quickly onto a zip drive and mailed it to his niece before he could change his mind and rationalize the deceit. She was his only living relative and he wasn't close to her. In fact, he hadn't seen her since she was a little girl, even when she had reached out a couple years ago. He was incredibly busy and never got around to returning her texts or calls. He and his brother were estranged and hadn't talked in years. He hadn't even made it to the funeral when he and his wife were involved in that fatal hovercar crash. That was an asshole move of me. Why hadn't I tried to meet her? Especially after her parents died? Too late now. Taking another deep breath, he looked at the fairy dance floor, took a few steps back, and then launched himself off the roof.

∼

BETTY-The Lost Scientist

∼

BETTY WOKE up on the street lost and confused. It was cold, but she had a warm coat on. Pulling it close around herself, she shook her head trying to clear the fog from her brain. A large venting outtake blew warm air underneath her from the building she was leaning against.

She whispered to herself as she pulled herself up off the ground and looked around.

"My name is Betty and I know an important secret."

What was that thing she had to tell people about? Something about smart phones and radiation... Then the thought slipped out of her brain before she could finish it. She wasn't quite sure where she was, but she knew she was doing something crucial, something that might change lives. She had been a lead researcher at The Corp but had been "offered" early retirement. She had started making noise about fears she had. Running her hands down her body, she noticed this warm coat had pockets. Sticking her freezing fingers in them she pulled out a cell phone. On the screen there was a big notification:

LOST? CALL THIS NUMBER FIRST. 416-555-6781

BETTY PUT the phone back in her pocket, she wasn't lost. She was on a mission. Brushing off the dirt on the seat of her flannel pajama bottoms, she took a look around at the deserted street and tall buildings. The sun was just rising up in the east over a big gorgeous lake. Or was it the Ocean? No, she was pretty sure it was a lake, just what was it called? She was going to be late for work. She was a scientific researcher... She wasn't sure where the office was, but a coffee would fix the fuzz in her brain. She started walking away from the water. What was she looking for again? She was chilly and hungry. What a beautiful old building up ahead! She stopped to gaze at the old stone and stained glass windows. Faded letters spelled out "The Cathedral Church of St. James." Pushing on the old wooden doors, they opened and she walked into the enormous building. The light trickling through the coloured glass took her breath away. She couldn't see anybody around so she went to one of the long wooden benches and laid down for a nap.

~

HONOUR- The Legal Prostitute

~

Honour looked up at the ceiling muttering, "Oh ya' baby that's great."

She was counting the thrusts of her early morning client, hoping he would hurry up so she wouldn't be late for class. Working as a legal prostitute wasn't a great choice for a part-time job, but she could make the most amount of money in the least amount of time. Plus, the hours were flexible enough for school. Her parents died in a car crash a year ago, just as she was finishing high school.

Unfortunately, her Dad had been more concerned with creating art pieces than saving money. He dreamed of becoming a renowned and rich creator of selfie environments. This art phase started about twenty years ago and had become a mainstay for museums in every metropolitan city. But sadly, he remained a starving artist. They subsisted off of her mother's construction worker paychecks. Enough for the basics, but her Mom had two dependants. They lived hand to mouth.

Honour tried to get in touch with her rich Uncle Frank, the CFO of The Corp. She hoped he could help her cover university tuition, but he never returned her texts or calls. A package arrived that morning with a little zip drive in it from him, but she hadn't had a chance to look at it yet. She didn't need data files, she needed Corpcoin.

When Dave was done, he hopped off her and threw his jeans and t-shirt on. Honour knew he was married and loved to complain that his wife "didn't get him."

She didn't like Dave's uber-male persona and felt sorry for his wife, but his digital currency was as good as any and he passed all the state-mandated health standards. When he left her apartment, she went to the window and looked down at the early morning view. She saw a lady wandering down the street looking like a toddler; not sure which direction her feet were going to take her, pausing to catch her balance. From her fifth-floor apartment she couldn't make out her age, or if she was in trouble. She thought about running down to see if she could do anything, but by the time she got dressed and hit the streets, the woman would probably be out of sight. Anyways, this new and modern city had cameras everywhere. A patrol would pick her up.

Betty sighed. The momentary distraction of the confused walker left her to confront how she always felt after a session with a client. Self-revulsion choked her. She needed money, but didn't she also need her soul? Every time she let some stranger climb into bed with her, she felt as though a piece of her died.

~

ISLA – The Rescue Worker

~

Isla started her shift at 7.00am and was scanning through the security cam notifications when she saw one marked urgent. She opened the webcam and saw the older woman walking on the sidewalk in the business district in a jacket, pajamas and slippers. Every few minutes she would stop and look around. Finally, she walked into the historical building that used to be an old church before the majority of the population abandoned organized religion. Probably a dementia case who wandered away from home. Isla opened a dialogue box and sent out a request to have her picked up. At least she would be safe and warm in the old Cathedral until a patrol could reach her.

Homelessness used to be a rampant social problem, but real progress had been made in the last twenty years. Isla worked in the social services division of The Corp and kept an eye on the city. Sort of a preventative 9-1-1 service.

Isla logged onto her social media site on HomePage and posted, "another woman will sleep in a warm bed tonight because of The Corp's vigilance!" She posted almost every work accomplishment and personal activity on her feeds. HomePage was her personal bible, journal, and most important communication tool. Though she had several thousand on-line friends, a breeze of loneliness was always drafting over her.

Isla didn't see any new alerts on her cameras, so she opened her Corp Love Connections App to re-read her messages from Samar. She had a real-world date tonight with him. Actual live human interaction could be the cure to her blues. They both swiped right a couple weeks ago. They texted and chatted like they'd known each other forever. Samar regaled her with intense tales of his homeland, India. She especially loved the stories he told of spirituality and how they practiced the Hindu religion. He defected here on a business trip a year ago and would have loved to find a girlfriend and settle down. His own Goddess Parvati.

ANGUS-The Alcoholic Paramedic

ANGUS WAS startled awake by his automatic blinds at 7.30am. They flapped up at the same time every day, he should have been used to it. He had not slept well, dreaming about the confused lady he had picked up yesterday from downtown core. She was suffering from delusions and may have been schizophrenic.

"Don't abduct me! I don't want to be prodded by aliens again!"

The memory of her voice still careened around his head, and he wanted to bury into his covers, not get up. The in-house Artificial Intelligence, ARISA winked its red camera eye from the ceiling above his studio's front door.

"You have slept for five hours and had three REM disruptions. Your blood pressure and pulse are elevated, Angus. Plus, it seems you drank enough alcohol to breach the maximum allowable amount last night when you had me offline."

Angus took a deep breath. "Morning ARISA."

"You should not be drinking quite so much, you are in Hypertension Stage One. You have a 3.54% greater chance of having a heart attack. Based on you being informed, your health insurance will be void if you have a cardiac episode today."

Angus rolled out of bed, trying not to grab his head and give away the fact he had a pounding headache.

"Thanks ARISA, I'll be skipping my CrossFit workout this morning. Nothing to worry about. Glorious day!"

"Angus don't try and distract me with the weather. I am concerned. If you continue to drink more than the maximum allowed amount of alcohol, you will be remanded to a treatment center. You are also losing a social credit for every poor beverage choice."

Angus pulled on his standard white uniform and got ready to go pick up his first "client." He tried not to be too irritated by the loss of social credits. This was a system originally used in communist China in the early 2000's. High social credit ratings helped you get upgrades in your vehicles, housing, and entertainment vouchers.

"Got it ARISA, no drinking tonight, put yourself on privacy setting please."

"As you wish."

He hoped he hadn't triggered any warning signals in the system. He'd had a couple of stints in the treatment centers, and he didn't need more group therapy and nutritional advice. He divorced one nagging wife and then The Corp started putting AI's into all new condo building units. Maybe it was time to move. If only he could divorce ARISA.

Nothing every really went the way he wanted it to. Angus had gone to school to be a content creator, but as soon as he was in his thirties, he noticed a change in the attitude to him at work. The Corp's business model called for young, cheap workers. Luckily, they funded many retraining programs and had been sending new career ideas to him on his feed. He saw there was a need for paramedics in the Community Aid division and it paid the bills while distracting him from liquor and beer. At least it was better than sitting in an office all day.

Of course, he didn't own a vehicle himself. You have to earn a shit-ton of carbon credits and social credits before being eligible to own a personal hovercraft. Angus had to use a push-pedal hover bike to get to work. He stumbled down the stairs to the basement to get his cycle off of the automated storage carousel. It took most of his concentration to keep his bike upright and moving in an almost straight line, when a pretty woman ran across the path. Angus swore and almost toppled when he swerved to avoid her.

"Hey Chubb! Get out of the way, you Pastry Puff!" Angus shouted.

Ouch, he must be crankier than he thought—way too much whiskey last night and shouting made his head pound even harder.

EMILY – The Cheating Wife

THE MINUTES COULDN'T TICK BY FAST enough. Emily was meeting her lover. Just because her lover happened to be a woman made everything a bit more exciting. Her husband Dave was so crass, so rough, and Darlene was the opposite. Soft hands, soft voice. She loved being with her.

She rushed out of the office as soon as it was quitting time. She worked the night shift at The Corp creating click-bait lists. Without looking she charged across the exercise path, her sights set on the coffee shop across the road where they always started their rendezvous. Just a couple of ladies having Cappuccinos.

"Hey Chubb! Get out of the way, you Pastry Puff!"

The cyclist was powering down the path using rage to fuel his locomotion. Emily jumped out of his way, shocked at his insult. Chubb? Pastry Puff?

She was a perfectly normal looking 40-year-old woman. A few extra pounds maybe, but really not fat. God, she hated men. At least, some men.

Pushing through the doors of the coffee shop, she saw Darlene at their usual table and was so happy to see her she couldn't resist leaning in for a quick kiss. Those lips and blonde hair. She was so beautiful.

Too bad she didn't notice the nosy fellow at the next table surreptitiously take a photo and post it on his public feed. When she got home, her husband was waiting, and he was not happy.

DAVE – The John and Abusive Husband

"DO NOT LEAVE your unit Dave Trumbull. The Corp Patrol have been notified and will be around to pick you up for questioning. Domestic violence is strictly forbidden." The ARISA in his apartment winked its red eye and informed him in her melodious voice.

Dave picked himself up from the couch he collapsed on after giving his wife a quick crack across the face. He couldn't believe he did it. His insides were so full of burning rage, his skin was cooking on his hot bones. Emily cheated on him. Some distant cyber friend of his snapped a photo of "two hot lesbians" at a cafe and he recognized his wife.

He and his buds back in college used to joke about how great it would be if their girlfriends wanted to get it on with another girl. Now that he was living it, it wasn't great at all. Maybe if he hadn't found out along with the rest of the world on social media, he would have reacted differently. Even worse, the condo AI caught his little slap to her face and now there was clear evidence he had hit his wife.

He activated his iWrist and called his lawyer.

"Chuck, hello. Ya'. I saw the post on Homepage. Ya', that's what I'm calling about. I may have given her a little love tap when she showed up at the apartment this morning."

Dave listened for a bit. His lawyer explained to him that he wouldn't be going to jail. First time offenders get rehabilitation services, counselling and a fee punishment. The anger management classes are held at old churches. Since the historical buildings are no longer used for weekly worship sessions, they have been retrofitted as community classrooms.

This system lessened repeat behaviour and actually

helped people get better rather than locking them up with criminals who either abused them or taught them how to be better criminals.

"Thanks Chuck. Can you meet me at Corp Patrol processing? I'm pretty sure I am going to be picked up shortly and brought there. Okay. See you soon."

~

SAMAR -THE COUNSELLOR

~

SAMAR DROVE around with Angus in his hovercraft when they saw a new alert pop-up from headquarters. Victim of Domestic abuse needed help. Counsellors often rode with the paramedics and this was an incident that needed a sympathetic ear even more so than medical intervention. They drove to the reported area and saw a woman walking quickly down the sidewalk sobbing and holding her hand to her head. They pulled over and Samar got out with a blanket and started talking to her in a soothing voice.

"Ma'am we are here to help. Could you stop for a minute and let me render aid?" Samar gently laid the microfiber heating sheet on her and she turned and cried into his shoulder.

There was something about Samar's soft accent and kind demeanor that inspired trust.

Angus stood back and dropped his mouth in shock.

"It's you. The lady on the bike path. Are you okay?"

Samar gently removed Emily's hand from a very black and swollen eye. She shook her head and didn't seem to recognize Angus as the fellow bellowing names at her earlier in the day.

Samar took her other hand and put a mug in it filled with hot chocolate and a mild sedative. He'd defected from India just a year ago. The streets were clean, and there was almost 100% employment in this new land, but it lacked the colour and passion of his home country. India was full of prayer, poverty, celebration, overpopulation, and lots and lots of life. Samar was willing to accept 24/7 monitoring and stop practicing his Indian religion for the chance to send desperately needed money back to his family.

"What's your name love?" Samar asked the woman as he helped her get into the van.

She stopped crying and looked over at Angus.

"Pastry Puff apparently. But when I'm not being screamed at by mad cyclists, I go by Emily."

"I'm sorry that happened with my co-worker. Perhaps he needs sensitivity training. Where is your husband now?" Samar asked.

"He's in our apartment, and I don't really blame him. Who wants to see their wife making out with another woman over coffee on the internet? I hear my post is viral."

Samar sat down beside her in the hovervan.

"Yes, your information file included that. We will take you for processing and then get that eye looked at by a doctor. Do you have any family you can stay with?"

"Only my grandparents, Betty and Darryl Bowmeister. But my grandmother is in the early stages of Alzheimer's. I'm not sure if my grandfather can handle another body in the house."

Samar consulted his chart and saw Betty Bowmeister's name on his patient pick-up list from this morning.

"Emily. You won't believe this, but we just picked up your grandmother earlier today at the St. James Cathedral. We will see her at central processing."

~

BETTY – The Lost Scientist

~

BETTY SAT on a couch in central processing with a nice warm drink in her hand. The taste was so familiar. She remembered it from childhood. What was it called? She usually liked it with marshmallows. Oh yes. Hot Choco. She loved Hot Choco. Why was she here?

"Grandma! How are you! Oh my goodness, are you okay?"

A lovely lady with red hair and a swollen black eye hugged her. What a wonderful smelling lady, and the warm arms around her neck felt comforting.

"I'm fine. Just remembering what it was like worshiping at a church. I have very clear childhood memories. But what happened to you dear? Who are you and why is your eye all puffed up like that?" Betty asked the lovely lady.

"Grandma, it is me Emily. Dave and I had a fight. I heard they found you on the street, apparently you were going to work in your pajamas?" Emily said, trying to smooth Betty's rumpled hair.

"I have some very important information dear. It's about people's safety. I just need to remember.... I must get there now. If you will excuse me, I have to find headquarters." A frown creased Betty's face as she got up and headed for the door.

"Sit back down for a minute Grandma. Do you recognize me? Emily. Your granddaughter," Emily gently took her elbow.

"I'm not old enough to have grandkids dear! And I do have to be getting to work."

Emily looked at her grandmother in frustration as she guided her back down onto the seat. She reminded herself it's not Betty's fault she can't remember things.

"Oh, yes, this is a really nice drink." Betty took a sip of the hot chocolate she'd rediscovered in her hand. "It was my favorite as a child. With marshmallows."

Samar came over and joined Emily and Betty with a warm smile. He asked Emily to walk into a little room with him and invited her to sit in an armchair.

"Betty won't be going home Mrs.Trumbull. We found her lost on the streets three times. Three is the magic number. Now she is going to one of our special facilities for society members with dementia. Corpcare Town is really amazing."

Samar popped open a laptop and showed her a digital pamphlet. "It is set up as an old-fashioned town and patients live in a non-confrontational safe environment. We don't force them to confront reality, instead, we let them enjoy their delusions and beliefs. Can you help gather memorabilia, photos and some of her favorite stories for us? We will decorate her 'house' with them to help as memory triggers."

A look of relief crossed Emily's face. "Of course I can. There have been reports about how highly successful your treatment towns are. I'm looking for a new job and would not mind working where my Grandmother is going. Working with people who can't remember the latest Homepage feed update maybe a refreshing change."

"There is a retraining program available and elder care is

a growing segment of the economy. Let me see if I can get you hooked up. Part of the reason I left India for the Connected Colonies is the 100% employment stats of those that can work," Samar said.

"You came from India? Wow. I have seen crazy footage on-line and on the news stations. So polluted, so many sick and unemployed. But the culture seems vibrant and gorgeous," Emily said, happy to focus on someone else's story.

"Yes, my people are fascinating, amazing, and free. But here in the Connected Colonies, there is next to no pollution, very little crime, and everyone has a job and is taken care of. The lack of privacy takes getting used to, but I think personal privacy is a price we are willing pay for safety and opportunity. At least that is a price I was willing to pay," Samar said.

～

HONOUR – The Legal Prostitute

～

COMPUTER CODING and Technological Sciences was a great choice for future employment prospects but could be mind-numbingly boring to learn. Honour staggered back into her apartment and collapsed on her couch. What she really wanted was a glass of wine, but the in-house ARISA monitored everything consumed and she didn't want her social credits or health statistics to be affected. Instead, she brewed some mint tea and finally slipped the zip drive from her Uncle Frank into her home computer. Oh my god, what was this?

It looked like a report on how the radiation from the new

super powerful smart phones was causing cognitive failure. Dementia numbers were rising in the population. Honour loved reading all the latest scientific articles that popped up on her feeds, and she had never heard a peep about this. How many hours a day did she have her phone glued to her head? It even stayed tethered to its charger on her bedside table. She was moving that to another room post-haste. Could this be true? She had seen all the ads for Corpcare Towns. The date on this research was a couple of years old, there must have been a cover up in action. The Corp made, sold, and created all content for smart phones. Someone at the Corp might have found the zip drive interesting. Somebody might have been willing to pay her a good amount of money to give it back and stay silent. A smile slowly spread across her face. She was going to call all her clients and tell them she was retiring. Then she was going to set up a meeting at The Corp. She was going to be rich, at least for as long as her memory lasted...

11

CZYKMATE PRODUCTIONS

eath Metal Fan

FIRST PUBLISHED: April 21, 2019
  Hauntedmtl.com
  Czykmate Productions
  Genre: Horror
  Founder/Editor: Jim Phoenix
  Pay: $2
  Previous rejections of Death Metal Fan: 7

~

Hauntedmtl.com

~

This website publishes horror news, criticism, and original fiction. Looking to learn about the hottest new survival-horror video game? Need some direction finding the best in scary television and movies? How about some original dark fiction? Jim Phoenix and his team keep the daily horror feed current and prolific.

Phoenix is an interesting and mysterious character. When asked about his day job, he said, "I used to write scripts and book adaptations but put that away once Czykmate started up. I do have 'another life' outside of horror, but I can't say what it is here. Let's just say my current day job isn't exactly 'open' about things."

Phoenix has some advice for writers looking to be featured on his site, "Be authentic. Make it real--from you. Don't retell the same ol'. Grab me. Make me shiver. Make me go HOLY FUCK DID YOU SEE THAT?! It all comes down to being real with your art. Hone your craft and send in the best version of that story you can."

~

How "Death Metal Fan" found a home on Hauntedmtl.com

~

THIS STORY WAS my second sale and I found the call on Submittable.com. I made $2.00 and it meant more to me than the bag of chips it could buy. The story is posted on-line and free for anyone to read. It's handy having a link you can pass on to your friends and family without a paywall blocking the way. I felt like it gave me some street cred actually having something "published" that I could link to on my website, Facebook and Twitter pages. It also gave me a thrill to see what the publisher wrote about my story.

"From scream down we love this..."

This was the first contract I saw with a monetary penalty listed on it, and I stressed a bit about signing it. It basically stated that if I had lied and this was previously published, I would owe — $1000. My story had not been previously published, but as any good conspiracy theorist would ponder: What if someone hacked into my computer, recognized the sheer brilliance of my possessed room fan story and stole it?

I asked Phoenix about this, and he clarified:

"Previously published can mean two things:

1) The author ripped someone off directly (boo!) or were using lyrics because they've seen their favorite authors do it (I think most people who haven't studied writing need a big lesson...ready for it...here we go: If you didn't write the song-- then please don't include the lyrics in your writing. Lyrics are expensive for rights and we don't have Random House's money.)

2) They published it before somewhere -- maybe with another publisher or even a blog -- and don't own the rights for a republish. Not owning rights to republish puts us in a shitty spot. Don't be that guy. Also, if you put something in a blog--and gave it away for free--why would I pay you for it?

Why would a customer pay you for reading something they just read for free? Writing is a business."

I asked Phoenix what drew him to "Death Metal Fan":

"Remember when I said 'grab me'? Check this hook: 'The weather was unbearably hot. Smoking, steaming, bra-dripping hot. Mia lay on top of her bed with a fan blowing air on her body. Moderate relief.'

Let's break that down. It's hot out. How hot? Smoking. Steaming. Bra-Dripping. Hot. Some writers ignore rhythm in their work, which is a shame--BUT--when someone does have a great sense of rhythm it shows up that much brighter. I loved the beats here. This play goes throughout your writing--'yada yada yada. Ya right.' That plays out as Bum-pa Bum-pa Bum-pa. BUM BUM! Alex Van Halen would be jealous of that rhythm."

~

Inspiration for "Death Metal Fan"

~

THE WAY this story starts is non-fiction. The true part: I was lying in bed on a hot summer night when I heard a party next door. I assumed the teenage son was in charge of the music because it was the most obnoxious death metal music ever. But when I got up to listen at the window and turned off the floor fan to hear better, there was silence. That awful sound was coming from the fan. I let my imagination create the rest of this murderous tale.

~

Lessons Learned

1) Having a story available on-line and free-to-see is a great way to market yourself and let readers sample your work.

2) I was experimenting with sound and cadence in "Death Metal Fan". A few of my proofreaders didn't like my sound effects within this tale, but I'm glad I didn't edit it out, because that's what Phoenix liked best.

12

DEATH METAL FAN

The weather was unbearably hot. Smoking, steaming, bra-dripping hot. Mia lay on top of her bed with a fan blowing air on her body. Moderate relief.

It was Canada Day and the firecrackers were ringing and lighting up the sky outside her window even though it was almost midnight. Mia had foregone any celebrations this year. She couldn't imagine facing 43-degree weather, plus bugs for hours just to watch different colours light up the sky. Whoop dee doo.

That's not all she couldn't face. Her boyfriend dumped her a week ago. The married boyfriend who was going to leave his wife for her. She'd hung in for five years… letting her late twenties and early thirties pass her by. Her friends told her she was being dumb. And she was. Another cliché. Another woman who thought they actually had something real. His wife wasn't kind to him. They were married in name only. Yadda yadda yadda. Ya right.

She didn't need to see the 'I told you so' expressions on her friends' faces. Or hear the saccharine empathy. It was all too nauseating. Her self-loathing was suffocating her. She'd always been able to catch the eyes of men with her long curly black hair and Kardashian curves, but the years were catching up to her. A few less construction workers were whistling at her. Less eyes turning at the local bars. So, she lay here wallowing in her sweat. Alone. Wondering if she could actually melt into a congealed lump on her bedspread. That would be the way to go. Mia missing. Slime ball found.

Feeling her eyelids succumb to slime state Mia fell asleep.

Until she was woken up by someone playing loud Death Metal. Her alarm clock read 3:00am in digital red. Who was having a Canada Day party this late? And who even listened to Death Metal anymore? Wasn't that an 80's thing?

She could hear the lead vocalist growling out "Give me a quuuuuuuuuuuuuu. Give me a yoooooooou. Give me an eeeeeeeye . Give me an ellllllllllllllllllll. And an elllllllllll. And a sssssssssss."

Being a fan of both country <u>and</u> western music, but not much else, she had no idea what band was playing. The lead singer sounded like Glenn Danzig from the Misfits after inhaling live flame. Here came the chorus again.

"Give me a quuuuuuuuuuuuuu. Give me a yoooooooou. Give me an eeeeeeeye . Give me an elllllllllllllllllll. And an elll-llllllll. And a sssssssssss."

Give me Quills? What an odd song lyric. This was ridiculous, how was she supposed to sleep? And didn't her neighbours go away camping this weekend so who was home blaring music? The properties in this neighbourhood weren't that close together, and she was sure the retired octogenarians on the other side of her weren't rocking out.

Mia unstuck her body from the sheets and crawled to the

end of the bed to shut off the fan. It was stationed in front of the window to pull in the cool air. (What cool air?) She wanted to hear where the music was coming from. Turning off the fan she listened closely... and heard nothing.

How odd. Did they just turn the music off? She couldn't hear anything. No talking, no laughing. No music. Nothing. Mia was stumped. She turned the fan back on and slithered back up to her pillows. She tried to find a dry spot. Laying there, she heard it again.

"Give me a quuuuuuuu....."

Holy crap. Was it coming from the fan? Mia quickly moved down to the fan and turned it off. No singer. She turned it on.

"Give me a youuuuuuuuu"

Good god. Her fan was singing Death Metal at her. Spelling the word Quills. If possible, she started to sweat more and felt her heart racing. She decided this was something she didn't want to ponder too deeply in the middle of the night. It was far too hot to turn the fan off, so she let the raspy voice lull her back to sleep.

In the morning, Mia woke up and listened to her fan. It was just a fan. Making a whiiiiirr sound.

Mia worked as fourth grade teacher at a public school in Richmond Hill and had the next two months off. Yaaaay. Her class had been full of nasty little girls being as mean to each other as only 8-year-olds could be. She had to deal with so many tears, she feels like she absorbed any misery her Kleenex missed. These two months would be a perfect time to recuperate. From the pre-teen drama and her own drama. But Quills. Why Quills?

Time to consult Google. The first and most obvious hit was that super creepy movie in 2000 about the Marquis de

Sade. Mia remembered watching it and feeling like she lost any innocence she had left. The sadism and masochism, the blood, and all the other bodily fluids that sick man played with. Yuck. Next was an on-line writing course for young students. Then she saw a listing for a bookstore near her. Just in Aurora, not a twenty-minute walk away. Maybe this was the Quills her fan was moaning about?

Coincidence? She had nothing else doing that day, so she swept her brown curly hair into a messy bun, threw on some jean shorts, a red I AM CANADIAN t-shirt and started hiking to Quills "the bookstore". The Greater Toronto area was still under a heat warning, so it felt like walking through soup. In April snow was still coating the ground, so she reminded herself to enjoy not being frozen to death and let the exercise perk her up.

It was a small shop with windows obscured by books piled up haphazardly on the sills. The front door was covered with pamphlets, post-its and advertisements for local events. Concert listings for bands with charming names like Death, Cannibal Corpse and Morbid Angel. Everything looked like it had been there for 20 years except for the shiny black sign "Quills" above the door. Mia pushed the door in and a set of bells announced her arrival.

Inside books were jammed on shelves, piled on the floor and stacked on tables everywhere. Most of the books appeared to be used, and that peculiar musty smell from damp paper was in the air. Science fiction, horror, and teen trilogies seemed to rule the genres. She saw lots of Isaac Asimov anthologies, Stephen King, Dean Koontz, and Twilight series books in her first perusal of the stacks.

"Ummm. Can I help you?" A nasally voice asked.

Mia looked around and sees a man with pock-marked

cheeks and hair sticking straight up on his head behind the register. The counter had so many books on it she hadn't even seen him when she came in.

"Just looking," Mia said.

"What do you need? I can make recommendations, I just got some James Patterson books in, some Suzanne Collins if you like the Hunger Games," he emerged from his book barricade and Mia saw he was tall and painfully thin. His Adams apple protruded and bobbed as he spoke.

"Why Quills? How did you come up with the name for this place?" She asked while running her hands along the spines of the books on the closest shelf.

"It used to be Pete's Place, my older brother's store. But he lived life on-the-edge. Live by the sword, die by the sword they say. Ha. So, I took it over. But my name's not Pete and I didn't think Irwin's Place sounded that great, ha-ha. My favorite movie is Quills, and books used to be written with Quills, so Quills it became," Irwin said as his nervous giggle trailed off.

"What happened to your brother?" Mia asked, hoping her sweat wasn't sticking her t-shirt to her boobs in a grossly sexy way. She could see Irwin talking more to her chest than her face.

"He was murdered a few months ago. A robbery gone wrong they say. But this place makes no money, so it never made sense to me. Ha-ha. Pete ran with a rough crowd, so I told the cops to check out his party buds, but they couldn't figure out who killed him. Wish we had cameras, he was killed right here. But no money, no cameras. Ha-ha," Irwin's twitchy laugh getting worse the more he talked. His eyes were now travelling the whole length of her body.

"Well I am so sorry for your loss," Mia said as she turned to leave the store.

There was no air conditioning and just one big ground fan stirring the pages of the books lucky enough to be in front of it. She was hot, uncomfortable, and horrified. The owner of this store was recently murdered? And she was sent here by her fan? She obviously needed to book a therapy session or ten.

She walked out into the even warmer street and was about to walk home when WHAM. A cyclist got creamed at the intersection. The truck turning left didn't see the man peddling across the road. Blood spray everywhere, and cars honked and screeched to a stop. The violence of the moment electrified the air. Mia felt adrenaline rush through her system. Her nipples got hard and a warm tingling started in her shorts. Instead of joining the chaos of bystanders rushing to assist, she turned and went back into the store.

Irwin was back behind his book wall.

"What was that? Was someone hit at that terrible inter-section again? Happens all the time," he said no giggle in his voice now.

"Yes. Is there a place we can go?" Mia said, pushing out the boobs she was trying to hide before.

"What?" Irwin gaped at her in confusion, actually bringing his eyes up to her face.

"A place we can be alone." Mia gave him a slow wink.

Rather than answer he rushed to the front door and flipped the sign to "Closed".

"Umm, haha, right back here," he said, his voice going up a few octaves and cracking in excitement.

Irwin led her into a back-storage room, and as soon as he closed the door, Mia took off her shorts and t-shirt.

"Okay, Mr. Hot Bookstore owner, show me what you're hiding under those shorts." Mia cringed at her own bad dialogue. Lord, she was going to have to get some better seduction lines.

Irwin almost tripped himself trying to get out of his clothes. Mia's pretty sure this scenario has never happened to him before.

Then she rode him. She used him. The thought of that blood, of the carnage outside, she can't believe how excited it made her. She bossed him around. It's was the most amazing fifteen minutes ever. Random sex with a distinctly unhot dude? Completely out of character for her. When they're done, they're both coated in a sticky sweat. Mia threw her clothes on and went back into the main book store area without even looking at Irwin. She stood in front of the big fan and let the cool air blow down her shirt.

Irwin followed her, pulling his t-shirt on backwards. "Uh, that was great. Can I get your number?"

"Don't talk. Don't ruin it," Mia said as she pulled her shirt and bra out to let more air from the store fan cool her skin. Irwin went back behind the counter but peeked out at her from behind the entire Twilight series by Stephanie Myers.

Then she heard it. Glenn Danzig but darker.

"Give me an rrrrrrrrrrrrrr. Give me an eeeeeeeeeeee. Give me a beeeeeeee. Give me an eeeeeeeee. Give me an ellllllllll."

Mia leant into the fan and heard it again. The faint growly voice singing out letters.

"Rebel," she whispered to herself. She doesn't have to Google this one. Rebel is the hottest nightclub in Toronto and it's right down by the lake. Without a backwards glance at goggle-eyed Irwin she walked out of Quills and headed back home. The poor cyclist was just getting loaded into an ambulance, but Mia wasn't interested anymore. She's planning her outfit for tonight. Time to go dancing.

Normally Mia's wardrobe is conservative. Knee length skirts. Modest necklines. But she felt like a new Mia. The kind of Mia who rocks a twenty-year-old geek's world and takes what she wants. This kind of lady wears a tight black dress. Short. Low neckline. She dug through her closet until she found some dusty dresses from her university days. Yes. She found one suitably sexy for a night at Rebel. With a bit of Spanx, this dress could still turn some heads.

She contemplated calling one of her friends to come with her, but they might not know what to make of this new Mia. She doesn't want to lose this bold adventure-y feeling she has inside. They'll think she's on aself-destructive rebound kick. (Is she?) She's no longer the scorned woman left by her married lover. She's a lady who's gone absolutely bat-shit crazy listening to messages sent to her by floor fans. She's getting turned on by bloody accidents and having sex with strangers. Later she'll call a therapist. Sign up for maybe fifteen sessions.

At around 9:00pm she left her bungalow and drove down to Toronto's Harbourfront. Finding rock-star parking on Polson Street, she strutted into Rebel's cavernous converted warehouse. Psychedelic strobe lights illuminated the dance floor and bodies gyrated to music spun by DJ Deadmau5.

Not sure what she was looking for and seeing no available fans ready to give instructions, Mia headed up to the mezzanine. After buying a watered-down gin and tonic for $8.50. (Good lord this place is expensive!) She sat down on a couch near a group of flashy club goers.

"So, there's lots of Blue Dolphin here, but how do I get myself some Purple Pete?" an Italian guy in a custom suit asked a blonde woman in a sequined tea towel on the couch behind her.

"It used to be you could only get Purple Pete from this place in Aurora. A hole in the wall bookstore called Pete's Place. But it was the best ecstasy on the market. Rumor has it he made it right on premises. But now Damon is holding some," the blonde said while wiggling on her seat trying to make sure the tea towel kept her strategic parts covered.

"Is Damon here tonight?" asked the Italian guy looking around and gulping at his Heineken

"Damon is always here," the blonde answered and nodded in the direction of a tall man wearing jeans and a sport jacket leaning on the mezzanine railing. The second floor of the club had a low glass wall encircling it so guests could lean over and stare at the writhing bodies below.

Mia watched as Italian guy walked over and spent a few minutes talking to Damon. The transaction was over quickly, and the couch behind her emptied out to go down to the dance floor. The second floor was basically deserted. Mia tossed her hair over one eye, hiked up her skirt and walked over to Damon.

"Purple Pete please," she said in her sexiest voice.

"Thirty bucks a pill," Damon said and ran his predatory eyes up and down Mia's body. "This stuff makes you want to party. I'd wouldn't mind partying alone with you later."

Mia flicked out her tongue at him and sidled closer. (She's rusty, so she's hoping tongue flicking is sexy.)

"Lean back and maybe we can do some partying now. It's dark and there's no one up here" she purred while rotating her hips in a suggestive way and doing another tongue flick.

Damon put his hands on his hips and leaned back on the railing as Mia knelt down in front of him.

"Oh ya, consider your first pill comped." Damon said as he zipped down his pants.

Rather than drop to her knees, Mia tucked one shoulder forward, thrust up on her legs, and heaved him over the railing.

If Damon screamed on the way down to the dance floor, she couldn't hear it. Mia's blood pumped quickly through her veins and a delightful shot of serotonin lit up her brain. Wow. What a rush. Forget Purple Pete, she'd take the Red Damon please. Red bloody Damon she thought with joy. Looking around, no one seemed to have noticed anything on the mezzanine. She walked quickly towards the bathrooms and back stairs away from the main floor overlook. What was going on with her? She felt like she did after riding Irwin. Powerful. Sated. Aroused. No amount of therapy was going to save her now.

As she climbed down the back stairs, the music stopped and the regular lights came back on. She could hear the shocked gasps and screams coming from the dance floor. She walked back towards the front of the club and joined the crowd around the sprawled man.

God, it was like art, the way the blood was splattered around his body.

"What happened?" she asked a couple beside her, making sure no saw that he was pushed.

The girl sobbed, "a guy fell over the wall and he's dead!"

Her date said, "this is going to ruin the party tonight."

Mia thanked them and headed rapidly for the door. She's got to get out before they decide to shut the place down and have cops interview everyone. A few other clubbers had the same idea and they all walked out of the front door together in the chaos and confusion.

Driving home, Mia held onto the tingly unfamiliar feeling in her stomach. She felt free, happy, corrupt and like a totally new person. Did she just avenge Pete's death? Was he the voice in her fan? That was pretty crazy to contemplate but strange things happened everyday.

When she got home she ripped off her black dress and hopped naked into bed. Even though the night is cooler, she makes sure her fan is going full tilt. And she listens......

13

NBH PUBLISHING

The Midlife Storm

~

FIRST PUBLISHED: October 31, 2019
The Killer Collection
NBH Publishing
Genre: Crime Horror
Publisher: Nick Botic
Pay: Royalties ($0)
Previous rejections of A Midlife Storm: 10

~

NBH Publishing

~

NICK BOTIC STARTED NBH Publishing in 2018, and produced a couple of horror anthologies, but has since turned his attentions to his personal writing and horror podcast.

100 Percent True

Nick Botic is one of those elusive authors who has found a way to live full-time off of his writing. A horror aficionado, he has gained a following of loyal subscribers who visit nickbotic.com to slurp up his newest scary stories. His latest venture takes terror off the page with a podcast and YouTube videos exploring Creepypasta called "100% True: The History of Creepypasta and Internet Horror".

Botic explains the term Creepypasta, "Funnily enough, I truly despise the term Creepypasta. To me, it just sounds like something that doesn't deserve to be taken seriously, and the people who write such stories (at least present-day examples) are nothing if not true, serious authors whose work deserves a serious look. But that's just me being weird and nitpicky. The term comes from the early internet slang term "copypasta", which itself is a portmanteau of "copy" and "paste", and is used to denote some in the Internet, typically short bits of text, that are spread via copying and pasting from one person to another. Once this started happening with short creepy stories, they became creepy copypastas, ergo, creepypastas!

As for why I'm drawn to them, I'm just drawn to anything horror. I love reading scary stories, and so many of the authors in the Creepypasta genre are just unbelievably talented. I like anything that puts good work on display, and there's no shortage of it here."

Slender Man is a Creepy Pasta. The supernatural tale of this gaunt, skinny, overly tall man with skeletal limbs is lauded as the scariest legend of its kind. Rumor has it that you see his shadow in photos lurking in the background. Sometimes he kills victims himself or he can compel others to murder for him.

Many of us writing and trying to sell our short stories would love to be full-time writers. Botic says, "Writing has been my primary income for a few years now. Since I blew up in 2017, I've been able to capitalize on my brand, which brings in a decent amount of money every month. As far as the YouTube channel/podcasting, I'm still working on monetization, but when it happens, I have faith that it'll be even more lucrative. In early 2017, I had a story called "Daughter's Drawings" go viral, and I just kind of seized the opportunity. I set up a website immediately and really just haven't stopped pushing my brand everywhere."

How "The Midlife Storm" found a home in *The Killer Collection*

I submitted this story to quite a few places before it got picked up. I used the weather to create beats and move the plot along but the true storm was its publication journey.

Before Botic picked up "The Midlife Storm" I had it sold to another publishing house for $25, but the contract made me very nervous. I'm not going to mention the name because I don't have any budget for legal battles. However, there was a clause after a bunch of lines stating you guarantee the story hadn't been published before:

"7.6. Should you violate to the aforementioned guarantee, you will be legally answerable, either civilly or criminally, or both, and in no case the amount of the liquidated damages is not less than Three Hundred Thousand (PHP 300,000.00)."

PHP are Philippine Pesos, and basically the contract stated that I would owe them approximately $6000 US if my story was previously published. Even though I was certain this story hadn't been published before, I had sent it out to quite a few places. The risk/reward ratio seemed high to me, so I struck out that part of the contract and sent it back. They countered saying the contract had to be signed "as is".

"We would like you to send the Contributors Agreement Form again without deleting paragraph 7.6."

I withdrew my story. Doing further research on the company, I found a warning about them being dishonest on a website called "Writer Beware", a good resource sponsored by the Science Fiction and Fantasy Writers of America.

Writer Beware

The moral of this encounter is "trust your gut." The correspondence felt a little off to me, so I am glad I withdrew my story. It was quickly picked up again by *The Killer Collection*.

Payment was listed as royalties. Botic explains, "I'm truly sorry to say there hasn't been much in the way of revenue from TKC. I attribute this to a few things - for one, we released on Halloween, which is, unsurprisingly, the time during which horror books absolutely flood the KDP (Amazon) bookstore. I believe that that is the biggest issue we've faced with TKC."

Fair enough. This writing journey isn't easy for the majority of us, and I applaud him for managing to get an anthology to print.

~

INSPIRATION FOR "A MIDLIFE STORM"

~

Do you know when you see a couple and their life looks just TOO perfect? Ever wonder what goes on behind closed doors? This short story is my answer to that question.

~

LESSONS LEARNED

~

1) READ YOUR CONTRACTS CAREFULLY. I'm glad I waited to have this story in *The Killer Collection* rather than sign something that made me uncomfortable.

2) Some writers actually do make a living from full-time writing! Botic gained his notoriety from having a story called "Daughter's Drawings" go viral. He says, "I get enough from the ad revenue in my website, which through the constant pushes of my name and brand I've been able to keep a steady

flow of people going to. On top of that, I do get paid for narrations and publishing submissions to various anthologies and publications. And finally, I have my books *The Things We Fear* and *A Halloween In Glarus* that get a few sales every month to bridge the gap!"

~

REJECTIONS

~

GRINDSTONE LITERARY SERVICES

"I think this piece did a lot of things well - the humour was a nice light element, the writing style was easy and engaging, and the fluid use of free indirect was a lovely touch, too. That's obviously something that comes naturally - the dipping from narration into the mimicry of internal dialogue - things like ACK! or when you said 'Speaking of Mr Freaking Wonderful,'. Now while those are good touches that can elevate writing, I think that the piece was held back generally by the tone it struck. Though it was well written, using capitalized words for effect, as well as placing this in present tense both make it feel like it was written by a perhaps slightly more inexperienced writer. There's nothing to say that work shouldn't include these things, but because of how they resonate with readers, one needs to be careful with their execution, lest they undermine their own hard work. I perhaps most enjoyed the resolution of the piece - it wasn't especially expected, and the abrupt end was a nice mirroring of the actual close of the arc. Saying that, the use of 'CRACK' in capitals really detracted from the maturity of it. I'd say reign that in, pull back from the capitalization, delve into the emotional depths of the characters more, and give us a human story to latch on to, and not just entertaining writing. Overall, well done."

14

THE MIDLIFE STORM

*A*ndrea gasped in frustration as she left the Mexican restaurant. Her Dolce and Gabbana suit. Ruined! One of her silly friends got too drunk, as usual, and spilled a tray of tequila shots on her. Some people just have no dignity.

She hated these bi-yearly get togethers with her old high school clique. They all sat around and boasted about how wonderful their lives were. Gag. Of course, Andrea herself put on the biggest show of all. Every hair in place, expensive wardrobe, carefully selected stories of work coups and how her privileged kids were out-performing their peers. When did they lose their authenticity? Twenties? Thirties? She remembers sleep-overs when they would pour out all their teenage insecurities and dream about how cute the boys were going to be in university.

Walking towards her Range Rover, she felt a sudden cool draft of air. It made her shiver in the warm evening. There was a low rumble and a crack of light burst in the sky. All of a sudden, a deluge of water was soaking any part of her body not already anointed by tequila. Ack! Andrea gasped and tried. to run on her really uncomfortable and super expensive heels. Jimmy Choo. Why couldn't Nikes be all the rage for desperate-to-impress middle-aged divas?

As she climbed into her SUV, she sighed at the puddle she was making on the leather seat. She hoped it wouldn't stain. How fun would it be to try and explain that to her husband? Thinking of Mr. Freaking Wonderful, she hoped he wasn't going to be home yet. With Frank's surgical schedule, she never knows when he's going to be around. Though he insists on knowing her every move, he keeps his routines on a need-to-know basis. Andrea used to fight with him about it, but he has a bit of temper. It's easier just to let him do what he wants.

Frank is a man of unyielding ideals and standards. It makes him a great surgeon but a suffocating husband. He expects Andrea to maintain a spotless household and keep herself looking like a Stepford Wife. The ruined and stained designer outfit was going to bring a scowl to his handsome face. When her appearance doesn't meet his approval, she's learned to murmur an apology and quickly shuttle into their marble designer bathroom to fix whatever offends. What she really wants to do is launch herself at him and scratch the expression off his face. The one she used to adore and now silently despises.

Driving home she can barely see the road through the pelting rain. It feels like a metaphor for her life. She can't really see where she's going anymore. Outwardly it looks like she has it all, but in reality, she's drowning in misery. Aren't you supposed to have it figured out by 40? But here she is, 46- with a successful chiropractic practice, kids, big house, and a doctor husband with the soul of the devil.

Though she's furious at the single friend who dumped the drinks on her, she is also envious. Lucy's so free. No husband. No responsibilities. No kids to keep immaculately turned out and shuttled to lesson after sport after lesson. The great surgeon's children have to be overachieving over-scheduled little robots just like Andrea.

Sometimes she just wants to feed them messy peanut butter sandwiches while she lounges around in sweats with fuzzy unbrushed hair and no makeup. But that would never do. If Frank ever came home and found a scene like that...

As the rain tapers off she pulls into the driveway and sees with relief that her husband's Mercedes is not there. She does she see her nanny's little Mazda. Maybe it isn't wise having a blonde 23-year-old flouncing around in front of Frank every day. Why didn't they hire a granny-type with Nanny McPhee moles? But Katie came highly recommended by the agency and they had hired her three years ago. Andrea's marriage hit a really rocky patch when she couldn't keep up with the demand of being a parent to four children, her part-time chiropractic practice, and sweating an hour or two a day at the gym to make sure she kept her toned MILF figure. She's learned what makeup to buy to hide bruises. If Frank's house isn't kept perfectly his volatile temper boils over.

Plus, Lord forbid she ever put on a pound or two. Frank would wear his signature scowl and start making subtle remarks about her slide into frumpiness and unappealing middle-aged looks. She knows she should have left him. But being a single Mom with four kids? She'd have to give up the fancy house, the expense account, and worst of all, her perfect image. Even her closest friends thought she'd won the lottery in life. Who wants to ruin that?

Asshole. Of course, he has kept his toned tall physique

and acquired a distinguished salt and pepper look while keeping most his thick hair. He's charming and solicitous at work and at all social events. No one would ever imagine that the perfect Dr. Frank Gilchrist likes to hurt his wife.

She has a quick shower to get the smell of tequila out of her hair. (Even though what she really fantasizes about is letting the tequila soak into her roots while leaning over the kitchen sink stuffing pizza into her mouth and downing a few more shots for good measure.) Always aware of her slowing metabolism, she didn't eat enough to fill her stomach at the restaurant. Four tortilla chips. One alcoholic drink. Half a Mexican salad. FML.

She wanders downstairs in a light designer housecoat over full length appropriate silk pant pajamas. Katie the nanny has the four kids settled in the dining room playing an intense game of Monopoly.

"How are you doing Mrs. Gilchrist? The thunderstorm scared the little ones, so I let everyone stay up a bit late."

"I'm good Katie. Do you mind putting the kids to bed now?"Andrea laughs at the chorus of protestations from her kids.

Rupert, the eldest tries to negotiate, "please just let us finish this game!"

"Nope up you go," Andrea says with a smile of affection. Her future lawyer.

Katie efficiently wrangles them away from the table and up the stairs to their respective rooms. Andrea feels a tightening in her chest as she watches Katie's pert behind in tight jeans. She's sure Peter can't help but notice the same thing.

Part of her hopes he is having an affair with the nanny. Then there would be less chance of him climbing into bed behind her and waking her up with that annoying little poke into her backside. It's easier to let him thrust away for a few minutes than try and explain she's got a headache. That might not stop him anyways. With a sigh Andrea heads up to their bedroom and sits down to peer out the bay window. She sees her husband pull in driving his mid-life crisis sports car just as Katie walks out.

She can hear the low murmur of pleasantries exchanged between them but can't make out the words. Andrea hopes Frank will stop in the kitchen to get a beer or go directly to his office to finish up some paperwork. Then she can be in bed pretending to be asleep. Going into the bathroom she starts brushing her teeth quickly but gives up when she hears his steps coming up the stairs. Frank walks into the bedroom.

"Andrea are you in here?" His low voice says. Uh oh, there is a tone she recognizes.

Andrea stays quiet, hoping he'll go away. He doesn't. He walks into the bathroom behind her and starts rubbing her arms.

"I noticed the kitchen was a little messy," Frank says as he pauses his rubbing on one arm to give her a little pinch.

Andrea screws up her eyebrows with the sharp pain, but otherwise doesn't react.

"I'll get to it in the morning," she says trying to keep her voice light.

"Did you have fun with your girlfriends? Because I noticed your suit in the dry-cleaner pile," he gives the back of Andrea's other arm a little pinch.

She tries not to jerk away, but a small grimace touches her lips. In the mirror she can see a look of satisfaction on her husband's face. She has learned the hard way it's better to ignore his goading. A few pinches normally satisfy him, but if she tells him to knock it off or tries to retaliate, things will escalate. They will escalate in a very frightening way.

There's a reason most of Andrea's wardrobe has long sleeves. She used to kickbox when she was younger. She can't believe she has become the kind of woman who allows this. At first letting him have control over everything had been sort of fun. She felt taken care of. But now... The feeling of dark desperation grows a little bit more everyday. It had been at her knees a year ago. The she felt it hovering by her belly button a few months ago. Now it feels like the darkness is in her head. Like reverse meditation. Instead of a warm light she's filling up with a dark hate.

"I have a kink in my neck and some sore shoulders. A couple tough knee surgeries today. Think you can help me with that wifey dear?" Frank asks.

If Andrea doesn't react to the pinches, they can almost have a normal evening. It's like a test Frank administers to make sure she is still compliant. Still broke like an overridden school pony.

"Of course, Frank, go take a seat on the low wingback chair," she answers and consciously doesn't rub her arms where sharp pain blossoms.

She follows him into the bedroom as he takes a seat. Outside the rain starts up again. Andrea starts massaging her husband's shoulders and neck. She can hear the low rumbles as the storm picks up intensity and starts counting the seconds between the sound of thunder and the flash of lightening. She learned this trick as a kid by watching *Poltergeist*.

"One, two, three, four five," Andrea counts to herself. FLASH. The lightening brightens the sky.

She keeps a steady rhythm as she loosens up the tight muscles along Frank's trapezoids. Another crack of thunder.

"One, two, three, four," under her breath. FLASH. She sees her pinched face reflected in the light in the window.

She feels her husband relaxing as her expert hands ply the fascia -finding the areas of resistance. A really loud boom outside.

"One, two, three," she murmurs aloud this time. FLASH. She sees how much of Frank's hair is now gray on top while staring at his head. His damn controlling abusive head.

The storm's getting closer and the intensity of the rain pounding against the window increases.

"One, two," she says a bit louder. FLASH.

"What did you say Andrea?" Frank asks. Another thunderous crack drowns out his voice.

She ignores the question, "are you ready for an adjustment, Frank? I think you need some aligning."

"One" she yells this time. FLASH.

Andrea adjusts Frank's neck. Crack. Crack. And the last crack? She gives it something extra. All those hours at the gym. She's pretty strong.

As Frank slides down in the chair, the storm is fully on them. The lightening and thunder flash and crack simultaneously outside the window.

Andrea smiles to herself.

15

BATTLE GODDESS PRODUCTIONS

A Tasty Festival

~

FIRST PUBLISHED: September 1, 2019
Demonic Carnival: First Ticket's Free
Battle Goddess Productions
Genre: Comedy/Horror
Publisher/Editor: Valerie Willis
Pay: None
Previous rejections: 1

~

Battle Goddess Productions

~

Valerie Willis works full-time as Lead Typesetter for Salem Author Services serving under the main imprints of Xulon Press and Mill City Press. Battle Goddess Productions is her small indie press and she has published a "Demonic" series of short stories, including *Demonic Household* and *Demonic Wildlife.* One thing I noticed immediately about these books is the artwork.

Willis explains, "We are an unexpected blend with paperback books that are a little more decorated inside than the average book. Authors are encouraged to blend and mix genres and we do our best to let the readers know what to expect."

Willis also writes her own dark fantasy paranormal novels including *The Cedric Series.* I asked her why she started up her own press.

"I wanted to traditionally publish in the beginning. It was through conversation with several literary agents that I discovered some very important things about myself and my writing. First off, I blend and mix so many genres that my work can be difficult to market and target the right audience. Secondly, they gave me resources and advise and set the expectation that my story was good, but if I wanted to self-publish, I would have to become a small press or entity that wasn't afraid to push out the same quality look and feel of the big publishers. With all of the good advice, I moved forward with the reassurance this had been my fate. Learning so much, and after much practice, I eventually opened up Battle Goddess Productions so that I may publish, push, and help other authors like so many had done for me."

How "A Tasty Festival" **found a home in** *Demonic Carnival: First Ticket's Free*

This collaboration was a fantastic learning experience. There was no pay associated with it, but the process and lessons I learned from Willis made it worthwhile.

Willis says, "It pains me that I don't have the funding to pay authors, but I am glad that taking the time to provide feedback, keeping the rights to publish elsewhere, and an opportunity to provide author copies to sell in person or at shows is at least some of the ways I try to make up for that fact."

The writing journey can be overwhelming. The more you learn, the more you realize how little you know. Not every editor has the time or inclination to help you take a story that almost works and polish it. Willis is one of those rare editors who did. She put a submission call for a horror anthology and suggested writers email her and pick a ride or attraction.

The call read:

"We are looking for dark & funny stories featuring rides, attractions, or even stands found at a carnival. From the ticket booth to the Merry-go-round to even the Freak show. We want them all! The story should span Horror and Comedy genres in some form. The darker the piece, the further to the back of the book you will be placed. Lighthearted creepy reads often start our readers off in the front of the book. Be sure to email us to claim your topic!

Suggestions: Guess Your Weight, Shoot out booth, Fun House, Tilt-a-whirl, Bumper cars, Petting Zoo, Candy Apple stand, Pie Contest, Clowns, Dunk Tank, Ring o Fire, Pirate Ship, Ticket booth, arcade, Fried Everything stand, Cotton Candy Stand, Cattle show, Swine show, Rodeo, Bumper Boats, Himalaya, Pendulum Ride, Ferris Wheel, Drop Tower, Gravity Ride, Roller Coaster, Enterprise, Simulator Ride, Swing Ride, Caterpillar, Devil's Wheel, Evolution, Fireball, Fun slide, Log flume, Mechanical Bull, Slingshot bungee, spinning Tea cups, Top Spin, Tunnel of Love, Zipper, Ball and Bucket toss, Duck Pond, Darts, Shooting Gallery, Plate Break, Whac-a-mole, Water Gun, Ring Toss, Basketball, and so much more!

If you want to claim one, I will start to build a public list of taken items/rides to help other authors aiming to do something in particular or different from what's been claimed."

I sent her a message and asked if I could claim "Ferris wheel". She emailed me back and I started writing.

The first story I wrote featured a haunted Ferris wheel. It had a Twilight Zone feel, but no comedy vibe at all. I decided to submit that one to other calls and start again. (See "The Last Ride" in this book.) I had a vision of the gondolas detaching and hunting for victims, sort of an Evil Dead idea.

Valerie initially rejected "A Tasty Festival":

"As of right now, it wasn't quite the right fit. The Demonic Anthology has set an unusual bar for itself where a good amount of humor and horror are needed. In this case, we felt your story didn't meet the quality we were looking for. The plot was lacking in several ways including feeling open ended as well as never pulling in elements introduced (Look into the Chekov's Gun aspect of storytelling). For example, you emphasized the characters excitement about being tall enough to ride but never circle back to it. You had a great opportunity at the end where the Carnie could say "look there, Girlie, you're tall enough to ride" and have her freak out. A lot of the prose was telling and passive voice and I would love to see this in a more active. You should have us actively overhearing Hudson's mom talking to her mom at the door as she just glares at her green soup. Have her dad burp at this moment, and her reacting in some way. Another aspect was the humor was lacking, but I feel it would strengthen as you revise the plot arc and work the story in a more active voice.

We would like to invite you to revise and resubmit, or perhaps send in another submission if you wish. You have until Aug 1st to do so."

I took all of her notes to heart and rewrote "A Tasty Festival" and this draft was accepted:

"MUCH BETTER! Great job tightening this up. Send me over an author bio and if you want, a picture. Thank you so much for taking the time to revise. I love seeing a piece strengthen and always want this to be a chance to walk away with at least some insight and feedback about your writing and/or story."

A very diligent editor, she went through my prose with an exacting pen and the final story was a much more polished and enjoyable piece. This anthology made it to print quickly, so it was the first actual paperback book I could buy. There was no pay for contributing, but I did spend $41.99 buying author copies.

~

Inspiration for "A Tasty Festival"

~

I love the image of a decrepit Ferris wheel. There is a "well-loved" ride at the Sunderland Maple Sugar festival in our farming community. Peeling paint, swinging gondolas, strange squeaks, and a grizzled carny helping run it. What if this old ride came to life and ate children? Rohl Dahl is a successful children's author and his books have ridiculously terrible things happening to his young characters. Yet, his stories are magical.

~

Lessons Learned

~

1) Chekhov's Gun is a concept applied to story writing that says every element in your piece should contribute to the whole. If you have a gun in the first act, it better fire before the end. Otherwise, why is it in your story?

2) Willis summed up a good bit of advice for all authors, "An author should always understand 1) There should be a tradeoff (money, feedback, free copy, gaining access to a network) that you are satisfied to get in exchange for the

amount of writing and 2) Exposure isn't all that, when self-marketing and newsletters can do so much mores for an author."

~

REJECTION

~

CURIOUS GALLERY

"Thanks again for your time and story. This one isn't ours, but I enjoyed reading it. Have you tried Unnerving?"

16

———

A TASTY FESTIVAL

Stacey sat on her porch waiting for something exciting to happen.

Life gets so boring in a small town for an eight-year-old, and she wants something more adventurous to do rather than just ride her bike. "Stacey, you run around so much, I swear you have ants in your pants," her mom says.

Though she has given her underwear a good look, she's never found any ants. She's about to go to the backyard and see if she can really dig all the way to Australia when a loud rumbling on the road catches her attention. Some large transport trucks are rumbling by pulling and carrying carnival rides. The noise makes her want to cover her ears, but her eyes goggle at the amazing cargo. A green dragon head grins at her from the back of one, its twisty roller coaster body in a heap behind it. The ugly head of a fortune teller leers at her from its glass box, surrounded by bags of enormous stuffed animals.

She jumps up and runs down the road after the trucks. That's right! This weekend is the Sunderland Maple Syrup

Festival, and it's her absolute favorite time of the year. The first weekend of April is full of cotton candy, local bands, frozen maple syrup on a stick, and of course the rides! Forget her silly bike, she is going to go on the Ferris wheel, the Spider, and maybe even a roller coaster.

This year she knows she is going to make the height line; she just had a growth spurt and eight is so much older than seven. She's sick to death of only being allowed to go on the baby rides. If she has to ride in a little choo choo train one more time, her brain will go right off its track! Stacey giggles at her pun and coughs on the exhaust from the trucks when another kid joins her.

"Hey, the Carnies are in town! The Carnies are here! They're going to sneak into your house at night and kill you," Hudson, the boy from down the street shouts.

Stacey doesn't like Hudson. He likes to tease all the girls and hangs with the tough crowd of hockey boys. His blonde hair is always messy, and he smells like old soccer shoes. Hudson pulls on her curly black hair at school and Stacey wishes he would just fall in a hole and tumble all the way to Australia himself.

Her Dad is a quiet man who was born down under in Sydney but met her Mom on an artist's work visa and got married instead of going home. He's a carpenter who creates kangaroos and koala bears out of wood stumps and sells them to rich people as lawn ornaments. He always has a booth at the Sunderland Maple Sugar Festival and sales of his creations are usually brisk. This is why Stacey knows she will be seeing all those rides on the back of the truck at the fair, the family never misses it.

Hudson and Stacey both stop running after the truck and stare at each other. She doesn't know whether she should run from him before he tries to give her a noogy or stick around to see if he pulls a stupid stunt. Last time she saw Hudson, he was trying to ride his neighbour's pot-bellied pig. It somehow ended with him in a mud puddle and the pig on his back chewing his hair. She laughed for days.

"Hey Stace! Come with me, I've got something super cool to show you!" Hudson says tossing his water bottle back and forth. "The coolest thing ever."

"Yah, what?" Stacey mutters, curiosity tickling.

Her brain tells her to stay away from the bad boy, but she's bored. Hudson is never boring. She remembers when he came running into the school gym during an assembly with baby skunks under his arms. Total chaos. It was awesome. The gym still smells.

"I can't even explain it, it's so rad, you just have to come," Hudson grabs her arm.

Well, curiosity killed the cat, but satisfaction brought it back, so she follows him.

"This better not end with me muddy, stinky, or bleeding, and I can't be gone long. It's almost dinner time."

They walk a couple blocks to the ice arena and a little playground. At the edge of the teeter-totters Hudson shows her the most enormous ant hill. Little red dots scurry back and forth keeping their metropolis fed and growing.

She knells down, glad for her tight joggers, she doesn't need any of these getting in her pants, "Look at all the darling busy things." Hudson walks away collecting little bits of tree branch and sticks. "What are you doing?"

Not answering, he piles them on the hole at the top of the hill. Digging into his jeans he pulls out a matchbook and lights the tinder. A bit of flame immediately catches with a small whoosh. The ants scurry everywhere, racing for their wee lives.

"Hudson! Don't burn them! That's terrible," she huffs at the flames, but can't seem to blow them out. She contemplates grabbing a few bigger red ants to slide into his underwear. Hopefully they are the biting kind.

"Firetruck 81, responding to a 9-1-1 call!" Hudson bellows. Picking up a water bottle he tossed on the dirt, he dumps the liquid on his small fire. With a hiss it extinguishes.

"See? I'm a hero," Hudson says proudly, "I saved the big ant condominium."

Stacey stares at him. She never should have followed a known sociopath.

"Hey, what's that over there? By the corn field?" Hudson points at a metal structure sitting at the edge of the field near last year's corn husks. She stands up to look, "I'm not sure. Doesn't look like it belongs. Is someone dumping garbage?"

They walk over to it, and gap at the thing. It's a square box with roll bars overhead and a pea soup green seat with torn cushions. Little doors are attached to each side with grotesque clown faces painted on them. Stacey is NOT a fan of clowns after watching Stephen King's IT one night with an overly permissive babysitter. Sometimes you think you are grown up enough, and you just aren't. She doesn't even like red balloons anymore.

"It looks like part of a Ferris Wheel," she says getting a little closer, "how would it get here?"

"It's cool," Hudson shouts, pulling open the little side door and hop ping onto the seat.

With a clang the clown face panel swings shut.

"BLURP," a big sucking sound comes out of the cab.

Hudson screams as his butt sinks into the seat. The green

cushion opens like a huge mouth and Hudson is now bent over at the waist with his legs and arms sticking out in front of him. He looks ridiculous, and Stacey wants to giggle at the way his eyes are popping out of his face, and the small "O" of his mouth open in surprise.

"Is this another of your stunts? It's better than pig riding." "Get me out of here! Get help," Hudson yells as he sinks in even further until just his shoes and hands are visible.

Then it's too late for help, Hudson is gone, and the green seat looked solid again. Stacey takes a few steps back. This is crazy. She didn't just see a boy eaten by a Ferris Wheel cab, did she?

"BURP", the green seat flaps open and shut.

She did.

Stacey turns and runs as fast as her legs can take her. When she gets back to the playground she turns and looks back for the carnivorous carnival seat, but the metal thing and Hudson are gone. She walks home quickly trying to figure out what to do about this. No one is going to believe her story.

Once she came screaming in from the back yard, "Dad there is a huge rattlesnake in the yard! It almost got me!"

After her father spent an hour searching through his gardens with a pitchfork and a can of Raid, she had to fess up.

"Maybe it was only a garter snake, it just looked like it was a rattlesnake." She was grounded for an entire week for something called "hyperbole." She's still not exactly sure what that means, but she knows her parents roll their eyes if she tells too fantastic a tale.

When she gets home her mother has dinner on the table, so Stacey doesn't say anything. She gags when she tries to eat the green pea soup. Visions of a little Hudson swimming around in the green mush makes her stir her spoon around trying to squash him.

There is a knock at the door, and her mom opens it.

"Have you seen Hudson, he hasn't come home for supper, which is unusual for him," the blonde lady with her hair sprayed into a massive pouf asks.

"Stacey, do you know where Hudson is?" her mom calls over her shoulder.

She imagines telling the two ladies that Hudson has been sucked into another world through the green seat of an old Ferris wheel. Her parents might ground her until she's old enough to go to university. "Mom, I have NO idea where Hudson could be."

Lying in bed that night, she half convinces herself she dreamed the whole encounter. She'd rather think of fun things, like riding the green dragon roller coaster! She falls into a deep sleep...

THE NEXT DAY her family packs up the van with a bunch of Dad's creations, and Stacey hops in the back with the wooden kangaroos, possums, and wombats. Hudson probably stumbled home last night after playing a mean trick on all of them. Imagine believing a nasty piece of carnival ride ate him! She helps set up the tables and sculptures, but her tummy is getting bubbly thinking about the rides.

"Can I go explore now?"

"Sure thing, honey, just take my cell phone and call your Dad if you need anything or get into trouble. Keep an eye out for Hudson," her Mom says pulling a toque onto Stacey's head. Great, now she looks like a cone head. If she lived in

Australia, she wouldn't have to wear silly toques, but the April breeze is cool and blows last year's leaves up and down the street.

She slips away, listening to the band warming up, and watching the big draft horses taking their first visitors for a tour in a hay wagon. A big pot of maple syrup is boiling by the old church. The sweet smell tickles her nostrils. The midway should be open, and she's got to double check her height.

The main town parking lot has been transformed into a wonderland of fun, food, and midway rides. Stacey watches the green dragon roller coaster clack by and can't wait to try it out. The ticket booth has the coloured height tester. She runs over and lines up beneath it. Yes! A Carnie with a bald head and toothless smile wordlessly hands her the bracelet that means she can go on anything. The line-up for the roller coaster and the spider is pretty long, so she walks over to the Ferris wheel, which has no one waiting.

The old ride towers into the air, with the metal seats with green cushions and clowns painted on the sides swinging in the wind. A cheery

version of "Pop Goes the Weasel" plays out of tinny speakers. Stacey comes to a dead stop, her heart threatening to jump up and run out of her mouth. She's afraid Hudson might pop out of one of the cars.

Another Carnie with a dirty ball cap and patched overalls turns and looks at her.

"Hey Girlie! Want to be the first one on? I see you're tall enough to ride!" Backing away, Stacey turns and sprints out of the midway. Maybe she's had enough excitement for the moment. She knows one thing is for sure, she is NEVER going to ride the Ferris wheel.

17

CORONA BOOKS UK

 he Last Ride

FIRST PUBLISHED: October 1, 2019
The Corona Book of Ghost Stories
By Corona Books UK
Genre: Horror
Publisher: Lewis Williams
Pay: $67
Previous rejections: 5

~

Corona Books UK

~

In 2015, these UK-based independent publishers had no idea that the word "corona" was going to become recognized world-wide. The unfortunate name coincidence aside, they have published a series of anthologies compiling brilliant and quirky short stories in the realms of horror, sci-fi and humour. Lewis Williams is the founder of Corona Books UK, and he says "As well as my work for Corona Books, I also do freelance work and have set up a business, Cavalcade Books, with a partner to deliver affordable, quality author-funded publishing services."

They have published three volumes of *The Corona Book of Horror Stories*, three Limerick books which promise "vulgar humour", and a single volume of *The Corona Book of Ghost Stories*.

Williams explains the origins of his publishing company, "A desire to seek out, celebrate and give a voice to some of the writing talent out there that mainstream publishers are apt to ignore. Genuinely, there's so much writing talent out there in fields like horror and science fiction. For our last horror anthology, we received over 800 short story submissions, and whilst it's true not all of them were of the standard we'd want to publish, there were still far more stories we'd have been very pleased to publish than there were room for in one book."

As to the future of this press, Williams says a name

change is in the future, "Hopefully 2021 will see a relaunched/rebranded version of Corona Books."

~

How "The Last Ride" found a home in *The Corona Book of Ghost Stories*

~

It was a bit of a struggle finding a market to accept "The Last Ride." Even though I was sure this was the most brilliant bit of writing I had ever done, editors weren't agreeing with me. The rejections poured in. Luckily, two of the rejections gave me some solid advice for tweaking the tale. (See below.) They both said it was a good story, but moved too slowly off the top. I tightened up the plot and brought the word count down. Then I submitted it to a call for *The Third Corona Book of Horror Stories.*

The acceptance email from Lewis Williams said, "We received a total of 824 short story submissions for this book, far more than we were expecting, and the panel and I were overwhelmed by this response. Nevertheless, we read them all.

Obviously with this number of submissions it meant that only a very small proportion could be selected for inclusion in *The Third Corona Book of Horror Stories*. It also meant us having to turn down a lot of great writing and a lot of stories we really liked.

We've thought long and hard about whether there was anything we could do to mitigate this, and we've decided that it would be feasible for us to publish a second book at the same time as *The Third Corona Book of Horror Stories* but which collected together the best of those stories from the 824 submissions that could in some way be considered ghost stories. This book would be called *The Corona Book of Ghost Stories*. And if you and the 15 others I'm sending a similar email to this to today would be happy with the idea, we'll make it a reality.

So, if I've not already made it obvious, let me say the panel really liked your story "The Last Ride". And if you would be happy for it to be included in the book, and thereby badged as a ghost story, we would be interested in including this story in our *The Corona Book of Ghost Stories*."

Hell yes I'd like to be included.

~

The Inspiration

~

I ORIGINALLY WROTE this story responding to a call from Demonic Goddess Productions for *Demonic Carnival: First Ticket's Free*, a horror comedy anthology. The submission call asked writers to choose a carnival attraction and I selected the Ferris Wheel. An avid fan of *The Twilight Zone* growing up (and I still listen to reruns on The Twilight Zone Radio Dramas App) I wanted to create a story that could have been an old episode of the TV Show. I also loved the idea of having a neurodivergent main character whose differences would ultimately make her stronger.

~

LESSONS LEARNED

~

1) IF YOU are fortunate enough to receive advice from an editor who's rejected your story. Take it!

2) I really liked this story, but had my confidence knocked when I received rejection after rejection. Don't give up on a story if you believe in it. Re-write, and keep submitting. Many editors have reminded me that just because they don't accept a story doesn't mean it isn't a good piece of work. It's just not what they need at the moment. Or they may have an aversion to Ferris wheels...

~

REJECTIONS

~

PSEUDOPOD

Thank you very much for submitting "The Last Ride" to us. It's an interesting story, but it didn't quite come together for us and we've decided to pass on it. I find Ferris Wheels super freaky so I was on the fence with this one. But in the end the buildup was too slow for a story so short, so I had to pass. I love your writing style, however. Please consider us again in the future.

THE MAGAZINE OF FANTASY & Science Fiction

(In this rejection C.C. Finlay references a previous story

he turned down. "The Writing Retreat," which was set on Pelee Island, Lake Erie, Ontario. See *The Publishers Behind the Pages* for that tale's journey.)

"Thank you for giving me a chance to read "The Last Ride." First, Lake Erie islands and now Myrtle Beach -- I feel like you're taking a tour of all my old haunts!

So I thought this got the feel of Myrtle Beach, and the story has an interesting character and situation, but it started slowly for me. I wonder if maybe Deidre was introduced earlier, allowing us to get out of Sabrina's head a bit and experience the story through their interactions as it develops, if the story would have more power right from the start, and then it would also feel like it was setting up the ending and Sabrina's choice as well.

Overall, the story didn't win me over for Fantasy & Science Fiction and I'm going to pass. But I wish you best of luck finding the right market for it and hope that you'll keep us in mind in the future.

Regarding your last email about "The Writing Retreat." I don't have specific advice regarding revising it or sending it out to other markets, except this -- no matter what anyone else tells you, trust your own judgment. You know what you're trying to do with your story. If an editor or someone else gives you feedback that makes you think the story didn't do exactly what you wanted, and you see a way to make it do that thing a little better, then revise it. But do it because it fits = your = vision of the story, not someone else's."

18

———

THE LAST RIDE

*S*abrina stared up at the abandoned Ferris wheel. It loomed forgotten on a run-down section of Myrtle Beach. It was impossible to tell what colours may have once decorated the swings sitting on the rusty frame. Dust and decay coating any memory of the laughing passengers of years ago. The crowds had migrated to the modern SkyWheel located on the popular Oceanfront Boardwalk and Promenade. It had a completely different feel to it. A metallic monstrosity which carried passengers in gondolas and soared an unbelievable height into the clouds.

Sabrina didn't like riding the SkyWheel. Being in a small enclosed space made her feel claustrophobic. Just one of the many phobias she dealt with on a daily basis. In fact, there was nothing she liked about the popular tourist area. The crowds made her feel panicky. At seventeen years old, she could be the poster child for mental health issues. Even now in March, after the school break crowds had gone back to class, it was still sensory overload. Cars blared music and cruised the main drag until all hours of the morning, some even with the modified shocks that made them jump up and down. Mothers hollered at over-sugared kids tearing up and down the beach.

A cool wind was blowing off the ocean tonight, making the open-air chairs rock and creak. This area was one of her favorite places to walk in the evening. There was something soothing about the boarded-up vacation cottages and decrepit boardwalks deemed not worth fixing after the last hurricane. They were damaged. She was damaged. Her ponytail had loosened and the strands were blowing into her eyes and face. Pulling the band off, she tried to tuck her hair back into its tight configuration. It took her three tries. Everything took her three tries. Every light switch had to be flipped three times. Her shoelaces tied three times. When she was typing her school work, she read over every paragraph precisely three times.

Her peculiarities really didn't start to manifest until puberty hit. As a child, they just thought she was quiet and shy. Then as a tween she became plagued with panic attacks and obsessive compulsive behaviour. Her parents hauled her to doctors and psychologists. The diagnosis was mild Asperger's syndrome, something they had missed when she was younger. She zoned out in the office when the doctor was explaining everything, so Sabrina googled it later. Basically, you have normal intelligence and language, but impairment with social skills and prone to repetitive or restricted behaviour. Yup, that was her in a nutshell. She did go to therapy once a week to work on her communication and develop coping techniques, but honestly, it felt like a waste of time.

How could she explain why she had to do almost everything in a multiple of three? She tried to give her mother and friends a physics lesson. How three was nature's favourite number. That there are three types of stable neutrons: The proton, the neutron, and the electron. And how all solid matter is made of atoms built entirely from these three particles. Science explained her OCD perfectly – one good thing she got out of high school. Everyone else was missing the logic. So she checked the lock three times after shutting the door. Brushed her teeth for exactly six minutes. Thirty-three strokes of her hair every night.

Of course, she got teased at school because of it, or just ignored. There were a few kids who tolerated her, and she even had one close friend who found her quirky and fun. Deirdre started hanging out with her in seventh grade, and never minded waiting while Sabrina zipped and unzipped her coat three times. Now they were both in grade eleven, and Deirdre's social life had blossomed while Sabrina became even more introverted. She had been invited out tonight with Deirdre and a few others to go to Applebee's for snacks. Sabrina felt ill thinking about the Friday night crowds at the chain restaurants. Plus, she hated watching the other girls roll their eyes when Sabrina started removing the ice cubes from her Sprite until there were exactly three cubes (or six or nine) in her glass.

Instead she was here, alone, staring up at a depressing amusement ride. She lied to her parents and told them that she was joining Deirdre for the girl's night out. Her folks were relieved whenever she put down a historical romance novel (her favourite escape) and went out like a normal teen. Her curfew was a reasonable – 11:00pm, so that gave her plenty of time to stride the deserted streets finding relief in the fresh air and solitude.

She was about to start her loop back home, when the Ferris wheel creaked and started to slowly rotate.

"What! Is anybody there? Is this a trick?"

Peering through the gloom, she couldn't see anyone at the base of the old amusement ride. In fact, there was a chain-link fence around the perimeter to discourage playing or climbing on it. The terrible creaking sound tore at her eardrums.

"Hello? Is anyone over there? This isn't a good joke!"

No one answered. Sabrina took a closer look at the chain-link and found that someone had pulled up a section just big enough for a small person to crawl through. Dropping to her knees, she slithered through the opening, swearing when a bit caught and tore her jacket. The Ferris wheel was picking up speed, and she could hear soft music.

Getting closer, she noticed the Ferris wheel wasn't as decrepit as she first thought. The music got louder, a fun jazzy piece. Then laughter and chatting. Sabrina closed her eyes and gave her head a shake to clear her ears.

When she opened her eyes, things REALLY didn't make sense. The sun was shining, people were milling everywhere and a five-piece band was rocking out under a big white gazebo. It was like a scene from one of her historical romance novels. The Ferris wheel was shiny with fresh paint and every seat was full. Ladies in frilly dresses, fascinators, and parasols sat delicately as they were whisked around and around. Kids laughed beside them, while men kept one arm around their dates and another on their hats.

Sabrina stood there with her mouth open. What was this? Had she slipped, hit her head, and was now lying in the dirt? Taking her hand, she pinched her arm, three times, hard. Yes, it hurt and yes, she was still standing in a world that had transformed itself into a lively and lovely day at an old-time fair. How many times had she read her novels and wished she could be whisked into the pages?

"Ma'am step right up! We have a seat for you right here," a young man in a colourful suit called to her.

The Ferris wheel slowed down and an empty chair stopped at the bottom. Sabrina hurried up the steps to the platform and took the young man's proffered hand. If she was dreaming, she might as well enjoy a ride. He helped her settle into an empty car, and shut the safety bar tightly.

"Enjoy the view, ma'am, and have a lovely day! We hope you stay a while," he said with a big grin and a quick bow.

The Ferris wheel started back up again, and it was glorious. The sun was warm, and the view was spectacular. There were no garish signs advertising tourist attractions, no big freeways, just trees and perfect little houses with the ocean glistening nearby. A small boy in the car in front of her turned backwards and waved at her enthusiastically. Sabrina felt happy.

After several rotations, the Ferris wheel slowed, stopped, and Sabrina's car rocked gently at the top of the structure. Must be time to load on new passengers.

A woman in the chair behind her shouted, "You can stay here forever if you want!"

Sabrina turned and saw a lovely young lady in a yellow frilly dress and matching feather hat.

"You can live here with us and ride the Ferris wheel whenever you want!" the yellow lady said.

"How can I do that?" Sabrina asked, feeling excited. She didn't want the ride to end.

"You just have to jump," said a man in a dapper blue suit from the front car. He must be the child's father.

"What? How does that make any sense?" Sabrina asked.

"You can stay here forever. We have fun everyday!" his son said, bouncing on his knees in the seat.

"Yes, stay with us Sabrina, join us Sabrina, we want you Sabrina..." all the riders on the Ferris wheel started to chant.

The sound of their voices and the rocking of the Ferris wheel in the breeze seemed almost hypnotic. What would she be going home to? A life where she was lonely? Where she never fitted in?

"Just jump, Sabrina, and you can have fun forever in this wonderful world," the yellow-dress lady said.

Yes, she could stay here forever. Like living in one of her books. She started pushing up the safety latch.

The voices got more excited as the sounds of the band faded. "Yes Sabrina, join us Sabrina, jump Sabrina..."

She raised the safety bar up once and brought it back down again. Then she did it for a second time.

"Hurry Sabrina, we are so hungry Sabrina..."

Her hand paused as she heard the voices chanting. Hungry? She looked away from the latch toward the lady in the yellow dress. Except this time her dress was ripped and black. And her face was no longer peach perfect with rosy cheeks. Bones peeked out from decayed flesh. The little boy was grey with teeth missing and one eye lolling out of its socket. Clouds had passed in front of the sun and shadows darkened the fair.

Sabrina gasped and shoved away from the safety bar. She had been just starting her third unlocking of the latch. The final unlatching.

"Damn. Too greedy." The ghoul turned back into a pretty lady and smiled at her. The music swelled again and the clouds passed on. "Come on Sabrina, you will love living with us!"

Sabrina pushed her body back against the seat and took a tight grip of the bars. She couldn't believe how close she had come to jumping. Would she have been committing suicide? Keeping her eyes screwed tight, she counted to twelve. When she opened her eyes, it was night again, and she was sitting in a rusted old car swinging at the top of the Ferris wheel. The people, the music, and the old town were gone.

She could hear was the whistling of the wind, and the distant roar of the interstate, but no brassy band. How had the Ferris wheel moved? If she wasn't a hundred feet in the air, she could have told herself she imagined the whole thing. She didn't have her cell phone on her. She'd wanted solitude so had come out without it, as for sure Deirdre would be calling her, telling her to come join the crowd. So, she couldn't phone anyone for help. There was no one on the streets to call to, and she definitely didn't want to spend another minute on this haunted contraption. Looking down, she saw that there was a complicated configuration of bars and struts holding the ride together. It looked climbable. Taking a deep breath, she crawled out of the car and slowly made her way down.

Where those hands plucking at her t-shirt? The metal was cold and rough under her palms, but she hung on tightly and scrambled down. A few little cuts started bleeding on her palms where stiff peeling paint and rough metal nicked them.

She thought she could hear a whispering in her ear, "Jump Sabrina, let go Sabrina, it would be so easy..."

Distracting herself, she envisioned the atoms of the Ferris wheel in groups of three and muttered to herself, "We have three atoms, which become six, which become nine, which become twelve..."

She still imagined cold hands and voices, but she could become completely distracted when she counted atoms. Grunting and concentrating, she made her way down to the ground. As soon as her feet hit the dirt, she scrambled back under the fence and turned around to look back. The antique cars swung slowly and hypnotically in the breeze, but they weren't rotating. Shuddering, she swore to herself that was the very last time she would ever ride a Ferris wheel. As she started walking away there was a whisper in the breeze.

"Come back Sabrina... we will be waiting..."

19

NOCTURNAL SIRENS PUBLISHING

A Bug in Amber Alert

~

FIRST PUBLISHED: October 25, 2019
Scary Snippets Halloween Edition
Suicide House Publishing
(now Nocturnal Sirens Publishing)
Genre: Horror
Publisher: Natalie Brown
Pay: Royalties $13.47
Previous rejections: 0

⁓

Suicide House/Nocturnal Sirens Publishing

⁓

I MET Natalie Brown when she picked up stories from both me and my mother, Della Sullivan, for her *Scary Snippets Halloween Edition* anthology. The submission call on horrortree.com read "seeking horrific short stories that feature the theme of anything creepy for the Halloween season. Ghosts, goblins, any and all horror is accepted. Word count: 500 words or less.

Multiple submissions allowed. Send as many as you wish and we will sift through them to pick the best for the collection. Exclusive stories only."

Brown is a fierce female voice in the horror genre, and a very interesting publisher to work with. She is approachable, candid and treats her authors like friends. Scary Snippet Halloween was chock full of stories, so I asked her how many submissions did she take versus reject?

"The project manager and myself accepted about 78% of all submissions received. It was our first and one of our largest collections. We wanted to showcase a little bit of everything and got a lot of really great submissions."

When asked why she has such a high acceptance rate, she explained, "The founders of Nocturnal Sirens Publishing were at one time themselves, first time authors. It means a lot to us to show people and the world how talented they are. So many new authors doubt their ability and talent; we want them to know that that's simply not true. We have published Mothers and Daughters (You and Miss Della) as well as a husband and wife who had never been published together before. Everyone has to start somewhere, we want you to start with us."

I also asked if any of her anthologies are profitable, "Our company gives 70% of all profits/earnings split evenly amongst its authors quarter-annually. Our two most profitable books are the *Scary Snippets Christmas Edition* and our charity anthology *No Safe Distance: Stories From Quarantine*, which raised over one hundred dollars for Doctors Without Borders in its first month of release."

She explains, "One thing I've learned is that the more authors that are involved in a project, the fewer profits are received by all. However, our company refuses to ask authors to submit for free unless it's a drabble or charity anthology, which we have had only two in the year and a half we have been making books."

Aside from her writing, publishing and voice work for horror podcasts, she is a stay-at-home mom with three sons.

She says, "as far as my writing background, I took a nine-week creative writing class in 10th grade. Besides that I have no formal training. I'm just a horror junkie. I've been reading, listening to and watching horror all of my life. That along with my OCD and lack of inner monologue seems to make me decently good at what I do."

Since the Halloween edition, Brown has also published Christmas, Easter, Sibling, Virtual, and Campfire Editions. Brown says, "I became a member of the online horror writing community in February of 2019. During that time, I have had so many ideas for future collaborations and anthology topics. Since then, I have been offered so many amazing opportunities as an author; I really wanted to pay it forward. It means a lot to help other people's dreams come true like others did for me."

~

How "A Bug in Amber Alert" found a home in *Scary Snippets Halloween Edition*

~

I USUALLY WRITE LONGER STORIES, but Brown's call for Halloween flash fiction seemed like an interesting writing exercise. I submitted "A Bug in Amber Alert" on Friday October 4, and received a reply two days later, "CONGRATU-LATIONS! Your story, 'A Bug in Amber Alert' has been accepted into the Halloween edition of Scary Snippets! Please review the enclosed contract. Even if you've already signed one; our goal is to have a contract for each story. In the meantime, promotional graphics are being made up to share your success!"

Brown commented, "'A Bug in Amber Alert' was one of the first submissions I read that stuck in my mind. Firstly, I'm a mother of three young boys, so anything mentioning the words Amber Alert automatically raises my heart rate. Your story had me captivated, I thought about it after I was done reading it, and it also needed virtually little to no editing. Kyle Harrison and I were more than grateful to accept it."

I forwarded the submission call to my mother from horrortree.com, and her story was also picked up quickly. This was the first time I'd had a publication make personal-ized graphics bugling an author's acceptance for sharing on social media. I loved having something professional looking to post on my feeds.

~

INSPIRATION for "A Bug in Amber Alert"

~

I LIKE the idea of how on Halloween, monsters and supernatural creatures could be walking among us and blend right in...

~

LESSONS LEARNED

~

1) THE HORROR community is a thriving and supportive entity on the internet. It's sort of oxymoronic that people who write such dark material can be so friendly and kind.

20

———

A BUG IN AMBER ALERT

*T*here is only one night a year I can effectively hunt for what's been taken from me. Halloween. When else can you go from door-to-door and peer in at the lives of your neighbours? It is also the only day of the year I don't get odd stares. Parents shielding the eyes of their children from my face. Babies crying if they do get a close look.

It's not that I'm ugly per se... If you can see beneath the warts and unruly hair that insists on growing out of them, I have quite a pleasant visage. Green eyes, thick dark hair, but I am plagued by those damn warts, and I can't pluck the hair any faster than it grows. My face was unmarred till puberty, so my daughter is still beautiful, her inherited proclivities won't be evident for a few more years.

I cast a spell of spider infestation on the neighbours who called child services. What ordinary human understands that dancing naked under the moon into the wee hours of the night is healthy for the young? I had no more luck explaining the late dancing to the government child welfare officials than I did the contents of our fridge. Frog nuggets, thistle weed salad, and newt soup are delicacies. They took my daughter away and placed her in a foster home, denying me visitation or even allowing me to know her whereabouts. Perhaps I shouldn't have flung vases, coats, and plates at them with my poltergeist incantation.

My local coven tried to locate her through lost and found rituals -but no luck. It's been almost a month since they took her, so I've resorted to old-school pounding of the pavement. Peeking in windows and flying above backyards has proven fruitless, but I have high hopes for tonight. With a bit of good fortune, child protective services haven't placed her too far out of my community.

Heading out the door, I join the throngs of little monsters, superheroes, witches and cartoon characters. The fall leaves smell like hope, and the wind carries the cool of possibility.

"Lady, great costume," a dad with three Ninja Turtles in tow, hollers.

I smile and tip my pointed hat. At each house, I walk up the sidewalk behind excited chattering groups of children and peer in as the doors open. Jack-o-lanterns leer at me in co-hoots on porch tables. So far, I haven't seen her ethereal face dishing out candy behind a door, or gotten a glimpse of the jacket she was wearing when she was taken.

Perhaps she will be out trick-or-treating herself? Skipping down the sidewalk with new school friends dressed in a billowy pink princess dress, or have the bones of a human skull painted on her face? I can't imagine she is happy being forced to eat the uninspired menu of the non-magical, and attending regular school. Spelling instead of spells, Math instead of magic.

When she comes into full power, her host family will be in trouble. But I have hours yet... the night is young.

21

TWISTED WING PRODUCTIONS

ersonal Demons

FIRST PUBLISHED: January 9, 2020
Strange Girls: Women in Horror
Twisted Wing Productions
Genre: Horror
Publisher/Editor: Azzurra Nox
Pay: $5
Previous rejections: 3

~

Twisted Wing Productions

~

Azzurra Nox is an avid fan of the horror genre, and this was her second anthology featuring an all-female cast. Her first anthology *My American Nightmare* had a successful debut and was published in 2017. Nox likes to showcase the work of women in a genre she feels is often dominated by men. She is the founder of Twisted Wing Productions, and also an author of a paranormal urban fantasy called *Cut Here*.

Nox says, "Some of the best ways to market the anthologies or any book, really, is to have it up on NetGalley as that will help with finding reviewers. If you don't have the money to pay for that then you can always use Booksprout, only you won't be able to receive as many reviewers. Book blog tours are another way to get your book out there. And don't underestimate the power of finding book bloggers and bookstagrammers (book loving influencers on Instagram) that focus on your niche, as they have a very powerful audience. I do a lot of marketing on Twitter too and have found that a lot of the preorders have arrived from there. Plus, if you have your own personal blog that has a decent following, it also helps in self-promoting. You have to be very proactive and seek people out in your genre. This can mean contacting indie bookstores that stock books in your genre to stock your book or newspapers or websites."

One thing that really stood out to me about this anthology is the absolutely striking cover. A naked dark woman with white spots on her skin has her back turned as she gazes out at an eerie tree.

Nox says she creates anthologies because, "By far, those have been the most fun to do because writing is a solitary task, but when you work with other authors then you're able to forge new friendships and I think it's important for writers to have friends that are writers too because they will be able to understand many of your struggles that your non-writer friends may not comprehend."

◞

How "PERSONAL DEMONS" found a home in *Strange Girls: Women in Horror*

◞

THIS PATH TOOK a funny turn for me. I mistakenly thought Azzurra Nox's company was Twisted Twin Productions. I researched the company and learned about the Soskia sisters, Canadian identical twins who write and produce gore-soaked movies starring themselves.

For months, I followed their Facebook page and even watched their popular film *Dead Hooker in a Trunk*. It wasn't until right before the release of the anthology that I realized it was Twisted WING Productions, not Twisted Twin. I had to start my research all over.

The submission call said, "Short stories should focus on a certain strange trait in a girl, whether the trait is physical (ex. Deformity), mental (ex. Demonic possession, telekinesis), creature-like (ex. Vampire, shapeshifter, mythological creature, mermaid, etc.), or supernatural (ex. Ghosts, banshees, wraith, etc.) or aliens. The author submitting MUST BE FEMALE."

I loved the idea of being included in an all-female anthology with strong female protagonists. I had a story in the works about a non-binary character who befriends a succubus, so I polished it up and sent it in.

My acceptance read, "Congratulations! Your short story has made the final cut to appear in Strange Girls: Women in Horror Anthology! What happens now? You'll receive a contract to sign and soon we'll get to editing (there will be three rounds of edits) and you'll receive occasional updates on the progress of the anthology and such. At the moment publication date is set for February 2020. I will let you know of any changes or updates!"

~

THE INSPIRATION BEHIND "PERSONAL DEMONS"

~

WORKING as an on-air producer for GlobalTV, I've spent ten years promoting the Big Brother Canada franchise. One of the houseguests in Season 7 was a non-binary person and they did an exceptional job playing the game. They were my inspiration for my character Sam.

~

LESSONS LEARNED

~

1) RESEARCH YOUR PUBLICATIONS CORRECTLY. I wasted hours and terrified myself studying the Soskia sisters.

~

REJECTIONS

~

GREAT OPENING. It immediately made the reader want to continue. Foreshadowing would have worked well here. You also missed an opportunity to build tension by showing these events (just a sentence or two) that carried the murderer along to the final murderous deed. The reader would then have been shocked but not surprised. But good use of the storm, the escaped detainee whose fate was underserved, and the decision to stay the night in the barn.

22

PERSONAL DEMONS

The locker was dark and smelt of old sandwiches and foot odor. Sam was small and easy to shove into the coffin shaped cubby. Tears tracked over chubby cheeks as Sam tried not to hyperventilate. Was the locker airtight? Was there an oxygen issue and she was going to die in here?

High school can be cruel. Especially when you are a non-binary student on the day your English teacher outs you. Mrs. Wilson had given Sam's essay an A+ and read it aloud to the class, exclaiming on what a wonderful teaching tool it was for fostering acceptance and awareness. Boston was supposed to be an enlightened educated city, but teenagers were basically the same everywhere.

Teachers could be so stupid.

Sam had written the essay on how they identified as both male and female. It was a deeply personal piece on the struggles of growing up not feeling either female or male, but always sensing both genders at all times. This was why Sam wanted to be referred to as them or they, and not he or she. Born with

female genitalia, initially Sam considered transitioning surgically but felt very conflicted. They didn't feel all male but felt
both the yin and yang. So, they decided to accept themselves as
they were. It was the final year of high school and time to stop
pretending. Too bad their classmates weren't as accepting.

"What are you Sam? A boy or a girl? You gotta be one
Sam, which is it?" Jeremy, the school alpha male taunted.

He had cornered them after English by their locker, a
group of five behind him. Jeremy was a tall physically
imposing senior with dark skin and super white teeth. Those
teeth looked like the mouth of jaws to Sam as his gang got up
into their face.

"She's got short hair like a boy, and she dresses like a boy,
but she's definitely a girl," his sidekick Caden sneered.

Jeremy's girlfriend Ling said, "You could be so pretty you
know? You should let me do your hair and makeup. Maybe
some fashion advice. We teach you to look like a girl, maybe
you feel like a girl," she said with a hand on hip bouncing
obnoxiously.

Sam whispered, "I have a right to choose, and you should
respect my choice. Just leave me alone."

"Who chooses to be weird? You are either one OR the
other. Not both," Donna added. Donna was your prototypical
blond cheerleader and BFF with Ling.

Donald rounded out the group and he was the worst of
them all. A fat red-headed boy with greasy skin, he was
popular only because he loved to fight and was a surprisingly
good athlete.

"Looks like you should have stayed in the closet Sam," he
said. "Let me put you back there."

Before Sam could react, he wrapped his meaty arms

around them and shoved them into an empty open locker. The metal door slammed shut, and Sam sat scrunched in shock trying not to cry. The tears came anyway. At least they hadn't cried in front of the bullies.

A sudden burst of bright light made Sam gasp and cover their eyes.

"I thought I heard someone in here. Hi, I'm Lilith and I'm new to the school. Do most kids hang out actually in their lockers?" The most beautiful woman Sam had ever seen was offering them a hand.

Sam grabbed it and got a good look at the rescuer. Lilith was almost double the height of Sam and impossibly slender. She had a full Afro of black hair framing an exquisite face with high cheekbones, slanted brown eyes, and a cupid's bow mouth.

Sam fell immediately in love.

"I heard about your essay in the hall. The whole school is talking about it. I admire you. Talk about brave and honest. You're not the only one who feels different you know. We are going to be fast friends," Lilith put an arm around Sam and escorted them down the hall.

Groups of students became quiet as they walked by, staring at the odd twosome. But Sam didn't care, they had a new best friend. The new kid and the non-binary person became inseparable.

A couple weeks later, Lilith suggested going to a football party hosted by Jeremy. Apparently, he had the hots for her, and dumped Ling a few days ago.

"Who wouldn't have the hots for Lilith?" Sam thought to themselves. Out loud, "I don't know Lilith, all the school bullies will be there."

"You'll be fine with me. Plus, I feel like I have to go. It's been a while," Lilith said, licking her lips.

"It's been a while for what?"

"Since I've been with a hot young man. A girl's got needs," Lilith laughed. "Drunk parties are the best. You can hook up, get what you want, no attachments afterwards."

"What!? You're talking like a dude. I thought only guys were into unconditional sex. I was sort of hoping you liked women. I am definitely more attracted to women." Sam said, disappointed. They had hoped their friendship might evolve.

"Nope, being a lesbian doesn't suit me. So, you will go with me? Friday night?" Lilith asked.

Sam nodded. They would do anything for Lilith.

SAM TOLD their parents they were sleeping over at Lilith's and the friends showed up outside the McMansion in West Roxbury around 11:00pm. It sat on a huge lot and big lamps lit the path to the front door. Music could be heard faintly and a few kids were sitting out on the lawn with red solo cups.

They went into the house, and Sam felt a little panicky at first in the crush of drinking, dancing and shouting. The smell of spilled beer lingered in the air, and music pulsed from a high-end stereo system. There must have been fifty kids with not an adult to be seen. Jeremy came up to them and put a beer in each of their hands. Lilith took a big swig and grinned at Sam. They just held their beer awkwardly; Sam hated the taste of the stuff. Lilith leaned down and whispered into Jeremy's ear and he bobbed his head enthusiastically, heading for the stairs.

"I'm going up to the bedroom with Jeremy, but I won't be long," Lilith shouted at Sam, "are you going to be okay?"

Sam felt a blast of irritation but nodded anyways. What were they going to do? Grab onto her leg and beg her not to leave them alone?

It wasn't a short time. Sam watched the football guys play beer pong on the kitchen counter and kept an eye on the clock.

"Hey, it's the he/she who doesn't know what they want to be!" Donald chortled when he noticed her.

But then keg beer splashed up into his face from a ping pong ball scoring a direct hit, and he went back to the game.

Sam noticed twenty minutes gone by, so they decided to make sure Lilith was okay. Pushing through the throngs of now very inebriated kids, they went up the stairs.

"Lilith, are you okay? Lilith!" Sam shouted over the music, but Drake's latest single was drowning them out.

They pushed open the closest door. It was full of jackets and bags on a bed. Two guys sat on the floor taking turns with a hash pipe.

"Sorry for disturbing," Sam muttered, not even sure they were noticed.

The next door was more successful. Lilith was sitting fully clothed on the side of a Queen bed, a naked Jeremy laying on the covers beside her. He was passed out, his normally dark skin pale, his burly chest deflated. Lilith had a satiated smile on her face. In contrast to Jeremy, Lilith looked impossibly gorgeous and healthy. Her skin glowed and pink roses blossomed in her cheeks.

"What's going on here?" Sam asked looking with concern at Jeremy.

"Oh, I forgot to tell you. I'm a succubus," Lilith said, standing up and stretching languorously.

"What?! A succubus. Like a demon?" Sam asked hysterically.

A low laugh trilled out of Lilith, "yes my dear friend, but you are safe, I only feed off men. I told you we were both different."

"Non-binary is not in the same category as being a soul-sucking demon," Sam said taking a few steps back.

"I only feed when I absolutely have to, my beautiful friend. Jeremy will be okay. He'll just feel weak for a couple of days and then shake it off. He kind of deserves it for leading that lynching mob that tossed you in the locker," Lilith gently enfolded Sam in a hug, "never let anyone take your power, you can take theirs, but never let anyone steal from you."

Sam felt warmth and energy as those beautiful long arms wrapped around them. Who was she kidding? Succubus or not, Sam loved Lilith, and she was their only true friend.

Now that Sam knew Lilith's secret, life got more exciting. Lilith persuaded Sam to get a fake ID from "this guy she knew" and they started going to clubs on weekends. There were always bars in Boston that didn't look too closely at their patrons' age as long as the money flowed. Some nights Sam went home by themselves when Lilith picked up a man. While Sam struggled with dark circles under the eyes and teenage acne, Lilith seemed to grow more gorgeous by the day. Her exotic height and beautiful body turned heads everywhere. Sam just enjoyed being in her aura, and soon her friend's sexual proclivities became normal to them.

The days (and nights) seemed to fly by and before they knew it, they had both graduated high school, Rather than go directly to college, the friends decided to head to the coast. Cape Cod was beautiful in the summer and Sam loved the well-kept cottages and sandy beaches. They took a short-term lease on a small cottage in Mashpee and both worked as maids at a tourist resort. Lilith continued her nocturnal conquests -never sleeping with the same man for more than a night.

Sam focused on trying to choose a college for the fall. They went on a few dates with a couple local women, but didn't hit it off with anyone. Besides they were still secretly in love with Lilith, knowing full well having a crush on a succubus could never end well. Before they knew it, November rolled around and the weather was about to turn. Mashpee was lovely in the summer, but the Cape was known for harsh winter weather. Lilith and Sam decided to head to South Carolina. Sam wanted to check out the College of Charleston, and Lilith was looking for fresh hunting grounds.

They started the journey in sunny weather and high spirits but after about seven hours on the road, the weather turned. Sam was driving and the skies opened up pummelling them with icy rain.

Sam tried to keep the car on the road by re-adjusting the steering every time they heard the rumble strips vibrate the tires. It was early evening and visibility almost nil. Lilith had her head on the window peering into the inky blackness. The rain was creating a cacophony as it bounced off the hood in waves.

"Hey, did you see that? By the side of the road?" Lilith said grabbing her friend's arm.

"What?" Sam shook her off in annoyance. They needed to focus to keep them out of the ditch.

"Someone hitchhiking. Let's pick them up," Lilith started whacking on the dashboard in excitement.

"Picking up a hitchhiker is not a good...whoa," Sam started counter steering as the car hydroplaned on the highway.

Lilith screamed, pressing her hands against the ceiling as they fishtailed wildly. Sam counter steered into every skid and slowly let the old sedan slow down. Regaining control, they pulled over to the side of the road.

Lilith was digging her nails into the upholstery, "oh my god, I thought I was going to die. That was insane!" she giggled.

"Can you die?" Sam asked, starting to laugh a little themselves.

"Yes, Google says the only way to kill a succubus is by trapping her in a mirror, but being impaled through the heart in a car accident would also do it." Lilith's giggle turned into a full belly laugh.

"You have some seriously dark humor," Sam said in shock.

Lilith's laughter was contagious and Sam started chortling themselves. Then they were both roaring.

A sudden rap at the window.

The laughter stopped immediately. Lilith and Sam jumped and grabbed hands as a dark face peered in at them, the night and pouring rain obscuring his features.

"That must be the hitchhiker we passed," said Lilith.

"Well what do we do?"

"Two choices, we either put the pedal to the metal and leave him in the pouring rain, or I roll down my window and see what he wants," Lilith rubbed the condensation off her window to get a closer look at the face.

"And if he has a gun, or wants to kill us?" Sam hissed. "Now that I know you can die and all."

"It's not that easy to take out a succubus," Lilith said nonchalantly.

Another gentle rap at the window and a hand started waving through the glass. Lilith rolled down her window.

A wet head leaned into the car. It belonged to a young man with a shaved skull and several fresh scratches. His grey jumpsuit clung to his muscular torso.

"Wow, that was some stunt driver stop, glad you pulled over" he said.

Sam braced their foot on the gas pedal, ready to roar away if there was a weird vibe from him. The guy was really good looking. Sam relaxed and saw Lilith go into flirt mode. The stranded highwayman had a very charming smile.

"No problem! What's a guy like you doing out on a night like this?" Lilith asked batting her eyelashes.

"Not the best night for a stroll is it? I have some family down in Florida and I was going to try and visit them. Are you heading that way?" he ran a hand over his head taking ice rain out of his eyes.

"I don't know Lilith," Sam murmured.

But it was too late. Lilith unlocked the back door.

"Get in! This weather could drown cats and dogs alike," she stretched over to the back seat to grab the handle and pushed the door open.

The fellow slid in. He was dressed head-to-foot in a grey jumpsuit and wasn't carrying any bags or even a backpack. Alarm bells went off in Sam's brain, but he was already in the car, so they decided to play it very cool. Pulling away from the curb, Sam kept a close eye on him in the rear-view mirror. He didn't appear to have any weapons on him. What does worry them is the standard issue outfit he's wearing. Was there a number on the back of it?

Sam looked over at Lilith to see if she's noticed they may have picked up an escaped convict, but she's draped over the back of the seat, flashing perfect teeth at the big man.

"So, introduce yourself, stranger of the night. I'm Lilith," she tilted her head at him seductively, "and our chauffeur here is Sam. I wish we had a towel to give you."

"I'm Diego, and you two are absolute lifesavers. Thank you once again for picking me up!"

Sam strained to hear their conversation over the rain. One of them should ask him about his jail house jumpsuit. It was like their friend was a mind reader.

"So why are you wearing felon fashion?" Lilith asked.

Sam listened intently to Diego's answer.

"There is an undocumented immigrant detention center about a mile or two from here. It is the single most horrific place you can imagine, they picked me up when I was surfing in Chesapeake Bay, so they made me swap my wet suit for this. I got tired of waiting for Trump to deport me," the smile dropped off Diego's face.

Up ahead on the road there were flashing lights. Barricades across the road, with the red and blue glow made blurry through the rain.

"Uh oh. Do you think those light up ahead are about you?" asked Sam.

"That seems like a lot of resources to waste on one guy from Mexico," Diego answered unhappily.

"No matter what they're looking for, as soon as they see your outfit, I think you're going back to that center. Or someplace worse. Is it a crime to sneak out of detention after sneaking into the country?" Lilith asked.

Sam made a snap decision. Turning off the headlights and wrenching the sedan off the road onto a little dirt path. Lilith screamed and Diego hit his head off the roof of the car as they careened down the uneven path.

Bouncing and shuddering, Sam frantically tried to keep the car on the narrow lane. The sound of the branches whacking the car made it hard to concentrate. Sam took their foot off the gas and let the car slow to a crawl.

"What are you doing? Are you crazy?" Lilith sputtered.

"Well either we save Diego or give him up. Maybe we can keep one guy out of Trump's clutches," Sam said.

"I'm not sure that was a wise decision for you, but thank you. You are what really makes America great again. Thank you so much," Diego said, the relief clear in his voice.

Further down the farm path, there was a big barn partially fallen down. Sam drove slowly keeping the lights off till they were at the wood and stone structure. All three of them agreed that it looked abandoned. One half of the barn seemed in fairly decent shape, but the back half had almost completely collapsed.

"Wait here, let me see if there is a safe place to hide the car," Diego said while sliding out the door.

He dissolved into the inky darkness and disappeared around the side of the barn. The rain finally seemed to be tapering off.

"Are you sure this was a good idea," Lilith asked when he was out of sight. "Are we criminals now? Some sort of harboring and assisting thing? Even demons don't do well in jail."

"I wasn't thinking. I just reacted. Here he comes," Sam said quickly.

Diego gestured at them to follow him, and they drove down a slight hill around the side of the barn. He pushed open a wide door and Sam pulled the car in. It had a dirt floor strewn with old straw and half fallen down wooden horse stalls along the wall.

Getting out of the car, Sam popped the trunk and pulled some blankets out.

"We can make up some beds and spend the night here. That roadblock will be gone by tomorrow morning. I hope. It was probably for a drug bust or something. Maybe it had nothing to do with Diego," Sam handed the blankets to both of them.

Lilith pulled out a cooler that was pre-packed with soup, sandwiches and drinks.

"At least we have some dinner. Let's eat and turn in. I'm sure everyone is exhausted," Lilith said biting into a steak wrap.

"I still can't believe you are doing this for me. Sandwiches and ice tea even. Who needs a fancy restaurant?" Diego picked out a tuna for himself.

He ate the sandwich quickly and then stood up and pulled off his wet jumpsuit. He had a pair of boxers on underneath.

Sam paused opening a can of soup with the big Swiss army knife they always kept in their jeans. He was built, a few hours spent lifting weights. Lilith's eyes glittered as she also checked out his spectacular body. Tattoos of skulls, roses, and bits of prose decorated his skin.

Oh dear, Sam thought as she pulled her blanket to the other side of the barn. They recognized that look in Lilith's eye. It meant she has her sights set on her next victim. Sam hoped she wouldn't drain Diego too much. He would need his energy if he was actually being pursued. Sam felt an affinity for him, he was quite likeable, and kept flashing them kind little smiles. Sam felt a deep wave of exhaustion and cuddled into the blanket falling into a coma-like sleep immediately.

Sam woke up as the first rays of sun came through the dusty windows of the barn. Getting up from the blanket, they walked over to where Diego and Lilith had been cuddling.

"Lilith what have you done?" Sam asked in dismay.

Diego was lying naked on his blanket with his impressive physique looking shrunk and drained. His skin was ashen. Lilith sat beside him with a languorous smile on her face. She looked spectacular; her skin blushed with vigor.

"Did you take too much?"

Lilith didn't answer.

"Is he going to be okay?" Sam pushed.

"I don't think so," Lilith said as she picked up one limp Diego hand and let it drop, "I went a little too far this time. I think he's dead."

Lilith laughed and jumped to her feet with the grace and power of an Olympic gymnast.

Sam stared at their friend. Their beautiful, gorgeous, friend who never seemed to age a day. Lilith stared back; one eyebrow arched. Just sipping from her victims and leaving them alive was something Sam could live with. But murder? Sucking a man dry and leaving him for dead?

Sam had an important decision to make. It might mean the difference between spending eternity in a fiery hell, or meeting Saint Peter at the pearly gates.

"So..." Sam said slowly, walking towards Lilith, "can you teach me how to do that?"

Lilith threw back her head and laughed, "Demons are born, not made."

Sam took another step towards Lilith, then pulled out the Swiss Army knife in their pocket and plunged it into Lilith's heart. The succubus' eyes opened wide, and a stream of gooey purple blood stained her chest.

"Why Sam?" Lilith sputtered as she fell to the ground. Sam stepped back, wrinkling their nose at the odd smell coming from the dying demon.

"You were right Lilith, I should never let anyone take my power, and I have the power of choice. Between good and evil, today I am going to choose good."

 lanet Nine

≈

Fɪʀsᴛ ᴘᴜʙʟɪsʜᴇᴅ: January 16, 2019
   The Gateway Review:
   A Journal of Magical Realism
   The LGBT issue
   Genre: Fantasy
   Publisher/Editor: Joe Baumann
   Pay: 0
   Previous rejections of Planet Nine: 10

~

The Gateway Review: A Journal of Magical Realism

~

From their website:

"Gateway Literary Press publishes collections of short fiction exclusively, primarily those with a magic realist bent. Because we are a small operation, we only publish between two and three books per year, so we are highly selective.

Our press is primarily interested in surrealist, fabulist, and magic realist stories. This does not typically include hard science fiction, high fantasy, or post-apocalypse and dystopian fiction, but collections of primarily surrealist stories with one or two of those sorts of stories are okay. Though we are highly interested in work centered on LGBTQ+ characters or written by members of that community, we are happy to read work by and about people from all walks of life. Due to budgetary constraints, we can only consider work from writers living in the US."

As a Canadian writer, I was lucky to get into this journal before they changed their submission policy.

~

How "Planet Nine" found a home in *The Gateway Review: A Journal of Magical Realism*

~

THIS STORY WAS ACTUALLY the first one that made it to print. It was a non-paying market, and a very interesting learning experience. In my struggle to get anything published, I had racked up about 20 rejections so far, and I was looking to find the magic formula for acceptance. It seemed most calls were actively looking for underrepresented characters, so I tapped into my fascination with a beautiful transgender acquaintance.

I found a call for *The Gateway Review: A Journal of Magical Realism* on Submittable.com and they were requesting magical realism stories for their LGBT issue, so I sent in "Planet Nine".

I heard back from Joe Baumann, "Thank you for sending us "Planet Nine". We would like to publish it in the next issue of The Gateway Review. If the story is still available, please let us know; we'll then be in touch in a few weeks when we start the publishing process."

My response?

"Yes! It is still available. I am very very excited! (I just started writing fiction in June of this year because of a broken ankle keeping me away from my day job and tethered to a chair.)

Thank you very much! You just made my day! (I normally don't overuse the exclamation, but wow, am I happy.)"

What was good about this call was the free contributor copies. When my first few anthologies arrived on the market, I enthusiastically bought the book or magazine for myself, my family, the lady next door...(you get the point.) A publication may pay an author a nominal fee like $15 or $25, but then I would spend over $50 or so buying copies. That's going in the wrong direction trying to make some money from writing. Now I keep a close eye when I submit to see if contributor copies are included.

LESSONS LEARNED

1) BEWARE of draining your bank account buying contributor copies. If a publication offers them, this is actually a valuable renumeration.

2) Featuring under-represented or neurodivergent characters can sometimes bring your story to the top of the slush pile.

24

———

PLANET NINE

"Hey lady! Get out of the way, you dizzy cow!"

The cyclist, looking like he leapt out of a Mad Max movie, punctuates his insult with continuous blasts on his iBike horn. Cora just about falls out of her hovercraft she's so startled. She <u>is</u> blocking the exercise trail but she had to pull forward to make a safe left turn. The exercise path just happens to cut across Corp property and she's trying to meld into the lunch traffic. There's always tons of activity down by the lake in Gaggletown's technical village. There's nothing dizzy about being safe. He's biking like a maniac, dressed like a kook, and going double the speed limit. Why is everyone so AGGRESSIVE?

"Look out for yourself! And cows are very stable! Not dizzy at all," she hollers at his sweaty back as he swerves dangerously around her.

She feels a red heat washing through her. What right did he have to call her a name? She's a perfectly normal looking 30-year-old woman. How is that cow-like? She's never understood testosterone fuelled rage. In fact, she doesn't really understand men at all, including her husband, Dave. They can't see eye-to-eye on anything, from dinner plans to their profile pics.

Cora feels nauseous as outrage mixes with the excitement and guilt churning in her stomach. It's her lunch hour and she's driving to meet her lover. Ruby. Beautiful tall gentle Ruby. So different than most of the content-consuming drones Cora rubs shoulders with everyday. Ruby talks about how important actual human contact is. How people are so concerned with their on-line activity that they're forgetting how to actually live.

Cora works for The Corp, the company that started as a single social media site and then grew until they owned almost everything. Homepage was the new FacePlace, except even more popular. As their profits grew, so did The Corp's portfolio. They bought every social media company out there and all the data that came with them. Ruby works for one of the few non-Corp owned companies manufacturing mobility devices for the physically impaired. They're looking to have targeted ads pop-up on a wide selection of Corp websites. Cora writes copy and produces video ads. When she was assigned the mobility project and met Ruby, she felt an immediate connection. Cora knew that nothing would ever be the same for her.

Ruby had been born male, but always knew she was a woman. She had the operations as soon as she legally could (The Corp policy makers deemed 14 was the age gender-focus would be clear). Their professional relationship turned passionate when they celebrated with drinks after the ads went live. Ruby lives alone in one of the small condos by Gaggletown's lakefront, so they always go to her place.

Cora knows the affair can't last. Everything is monitored.

Cell phones have tracking devices, but thankfully you can turn off the "find me" option in settings for now. The next upgrade will continuously track everyone. It will be like the meWrist and always on the grid (thankfully the operation to have an meWrist surgically inset made Cora queasy and she never installed one). Most vehicles have GPS unless you can find one built before 2020. The entire populace films and posts everything... There's no privacy in today's society.

Cora maneuvers her hovercraft down Alihaha Drive and grabs one of the blue P parking spots right outside Ruby's building. Ruby works at an office within 10 minutes walking distance, so it's easy for her to go home for "lunch". Blue P is of course The Corp owned parking app. Her husband does question why Cora has to drive 20 minutes to get lunch every-day. He can see all of their mutual transactions on-line. Cora told him she was addicted to this one particular shawarma shop. (Conveniently next door to Ruby's place) She always hurriedly grabs one on her way back to work so the purchase will show up on their CorpCoin account.

She runs up the stairs and uses their special knock on the door of apartment 207.

"Well hello gorgeous, come on in..." Ruby says as she opens the door dressed in a smile and nothing else.

"I missed you so much!"

Cora falls into her muscular arms and for the next half-hour doesn't think about cows, aggressive cyclists or her husband.

"You know we will get caught." Cora whispers as they cuddle under the sheets in post-coital bliss.

"Does it matter? You don't have kids with Dave. Just be true to yourself. You love who you love."

"I feel stuck, I want to be here with you, but I don't know

if I can leave Dave. I couldn't stand the on-line shaming. If you get labeled a cheater on Homepage, the trolls come out in droves."

Ruby pulls Cora close to her and grabs her cell phone off the bedside table. She quickly takes a selfie of their entwined bodies and hits "post to Homepage".

"What!" Cora screams as she hops out of bed in total shock. "What did you just do? I can't believe you did that?! Why, what? Ruby! RUBY!"

Her lover sits up casually and pulls the blanket around her naked body. "I did it for you. Now it's out there, and you don't have to worry about being caught. It's already happened. I just gave you freedom. Freedom to choose without fear."

Cora gapes at the woman who just betrayed her while quickly pulling on her clothes. Panic and adrenaline race through her system and she can't even stutter out a reply. Instead she runs out the door. She doesn't even bother stopping to get her alibi shawarma.

It's the age of self-policing. If anyone gets photographed or videoed using a plastic bag, straw or non-reusable food container the special interest groups write vicious diatribes and share the post everywhere. Likewise, being a spouse caught cheating, a bad nanny, or providing bad customer service. Your reputation is destroyed instantly along with your quality of life.

How is she going to live in Gaggletown now? Can she even go home? As she hops onto her hovercraft and wipes away the tears an idea comes to her. Instead of going back to work or home, she drives deeper into the downtown core. She has seen the videoboards along the highways and the pop-up ads on her feed. They are asking for female volunteers to live on Planet Nine as ambassadors. The native Niners love being in the company of human women. The space program has grown with leaps and bounds over the last 40 years. They've discovered there is sentient life on some other planets. Planet Nine has a thriving population with possibilities for terraforming part of it for humans.

The recruitment office isn't busy, so she's able to go through the questionnaire and health check quickly.

"You have very auspicious timing. The next shuttle leaves this very evening and we have a couple unfilled spots." The bushy black-haired man behind the desk says.

"I don't have any luggage," says Cora.

"That's alright, many of our volunteers travel light. You will be given everything you need when you reach Planet Nine. You will be treated like a queen over there! A car is ready to take you to the airport now."

Cora sits in the lounge at the International Spaceport, unable to believe she's here. It's the VIP room, so even though the spaceport can accommodate many thousands at the time, this comfortable lounge has about 20 chairs. She's ignoring the constant buzzing from her phone. The call display says 35 missed calls from Dave, and dozens from her other friends. They obviously want some explanation for why she's on Homepage in bed with a woman.

Eighteen of the 20 plush seats are filled with nervous looking ladies. All of them are attractive and look to be between 20-30 years old with carry-on bags clenched near them. Most stare off into space or bang away on their meWrists sending texts or doing last-minute internet surfing. (There will be no connection once they are cosmos bound.)

Two seats away she catches the eye of a woman who

would be pretty if she didn't look so wild-eyed and dressed haphazardly.

"Hi, I'm Cora."

"I'm Heather. So these are the voyages of crazy ladies running from earth! Boldly going where no man is allowed to go."

Cora laughs, "I love classic Star Trek movies too. But I didn't know men aren't allowed? Even thought the recruitment ads do specifically ask for women."

"I think the Niners identify more with female characteristics. The video ad shows them covered with a soft fur on their pear-shaped bodies and hypnotic gentle eyes. Something about them calls to me."

Cora says, "We are only the second shuttle, right?"

"Yes, I follow the Homepage of one of the first women to go and it looks like a fabulous life. It's a very nurturing world with no gender conflict. The Niners reproduce asexually. As a life cycle finishes, the organism breaks down and regenerates in infant form."

Cora nods in agreement. She had done some research when she first learned about the discovery of life on another planet. Because of the Niner's one-to-one reproductive practice, the population stays constant, and the actual livable land on Planet Nine, which is 10x the size of earth is immense. There's lots of room for more inhabitants. When the first earth explorers arrived, they were greeted with open arms. But as the contact between the two species continued, it became clear that the natives far preferred the female crew members.

She was mulling on what the male astronauts had done to make the Niners not like them, when Heather leaned over.

"Do you ever walk across a bridge and think about

throwing yourself off? Or drive your car down the road and see a cliff or big drop and just want to drive right off the edge?" She peers with intense concentration into Cora's face.

Cora's not sure how they took this abrupt conversational left turn. "I guess everyone thinks about that once in a while. How easy it could be? Like what would happen if an uncontrollable impulse overcame you and you just did it?"

"That's not what I mean. I want to. I actually want to jump off the bridge or drive off the cliff."

"I guess we are both jumping off the cliff. We are moving to Planet Nine."

"Are you married? Or in a serious relationship?" Heather asks.

Cora decides to be truthful with this lady who's just admitted she's suicidal. "Yes. Both. With two different people."

Heather barks out a laugh. "We are sort of alike then. My husband and I, we had these best friends. Chris and Kim. We did everything with them. Parties every weekend. Barbecues during the week. We drank. Smoked up. Hung out. It was perfect. Chris and Ken were best friends. Kim and I were best friends."

Cora interrupted, "Your husband is Ken?"

"Yes, if you like golden oldie television Ken is a lot like Seinfeld's George Costanza. But Chris, now Chris is more of a leading man. Works in insurance for The Corp's life and accident division. One day he stopped by my apartment without Kim. When Ken was still at work. And then he told me..." Heather trailed off.

"Told you what?" said Cora. "She knew why she was getting onto this shuttle into the unknown. It was interesting to hear why another woman was doing the same."

"That he was in love with me. That he had been in love with me for a while and didn't want to hide it anymore."

"And what did you do about that? That is a tough place! Did you tell Kim? Or Ken?" asks Cora.

"Well, I had feelings for him too. He was so good-looking. He had so much money. And I was so flattered that he was paying attention to me. I just went with it. I started meeting him on the sly. In parking lots. In parks. We would make out, have sex in the car. Really it was dirty. About sex, not about love. But at the time, I thought I was in love."

Heather's voice becomes strained, "we started talking, about how we could be happy and together if only something would happen to our partners. If Kim and Ken would just die. Or disappear. I never took it seriously. I thought we were just... making fun. Talking, like foreplay before the act you know?"

Cora nods.

"Then it happened. Kim died."

Cora gasps, "what?"

"She died. She fell down the stairs in the big home they had just bought. It was in the morning at like 10:00am during the week. When she shouldn't have been home. And they said she was drunk. Kim never drank in the day. And Chris. Of course, he knows all the ins and outs of insurance. He had a big policy out on her. He had just raised it recently."

"Was he arrested? That seems crazy suspicious? Did you tell the police that you had joked about killing your spouses?"

"No. I couldn't go to the police. I just couldn't. Ken doesn't know. He can't know. Plus, maybe Chris didn't do it. But I just can't help but feel he did, but I have no proof. The cops investigated but they couldn't find anything. It went down as a tragic accident. That funeral was the worst thing I have ever lived through. And Ken? I can't even look at him. I haven't talked to him. I can't talk to him. So... I am here. I deserve whatever is waiting for me over there." Heather finishes.

A loud buzzer rings through the lobby. The women start fidgeting and gathering up their things as the big door leading to the space shuttle ramp opens. It's time.

Cora picks up her bag, thinking of Heather's reason for going. Love, betrayal, and the inability to face consequences. She's right. They are alike. Heather's story was so engrossing, she hadn't had time to torture herself with the fallout from Ruby's post. She hadn't checked her Homepage feed or any social sites for that matter. She's never going to check them again. There is no internet on Planet Nine.

25

BONUS STORY

ℱarmyard Follies

❧

First published: March 26, 2020
Self Published on Smashwords
As Angelique Fawns
Income: 0 cents (I offered it for free)
Full & Sample Downloads: 28
In User Libraries: 2
Previous rejections: 17

∽

Why I tried self-publishing

∽

I believe this is the cutest, most well-written story I have ever crafted. My sister agreed with me. My mother agreed with me. No one else agreed. I could not find a market to buy this story about magical singing chickens. *The Story Behind the Stories* isn't a book about self-publishing and there certainly are some fantastic tomes out there to teach writers how to do the indie thing. However, I did self-publish *The Story Behind the Stories,* and I had to start learning the ropes somehow.

Kindle Unlimited versus publishing wide; Draft 2 Digital vs. Smashwords; Ingram Spark vs Amazon's print services; author websites; Canva; mailing lists; audio books; Bookbub; Story Origin; ARC readers; on and on and on. It makes you want to run screaming into the ether. I'm still trying to figure out the maze of things I need to learn. (If this book actually makes it into your hands, I have figured some of it out.)

I did manage to upload "Farmyard Follies" to Smashwords, and a few strangers sampled it. Twenty-eight to be exact.

∽

The inspiration behind "Farmyard Follies"

∽

I WROTE this story responding to a call on horrortree.com for *Across The Universe: Tales of Alternative Beatles.* The submission read:

"The theme of the anthology is "The Beatles – What if?" What if Brian Epstein hadn't managed the band? What if George Harrison hated sitar music? What if Ringo had been the true star of the band all along? What if the Beatles had been aliens? Or magic users? Or zombies? Or American?"

I crafted this tale as if my chickens were The Beatles. When it was rejected, I rewrote it giving my chickens the names of The Supremes. I figured hens should have female names instead of male

~

LESSONS LEARNED

~

1) I HAVE a newfound admiration for all the indie writers out there making a go of it. It is a complicated, ever-changing world. The very best resource for those trying to figure it out is Joanna Penn. Her podcast is a gold mine, *The Creative Penn Podcast.* She will also actually answer questions on twitter @thecreativepenn.

2) Repurposing stories written for one submission call often doesn't work for any other. I tried to shoe horn this story and make it fit somewhere else. It never did.

3) One of my techniques for helping my submissions stand out is to make a personal comment directed at the editor in my cover letter. (See first rejection below) Everyone

likes compliments, so I take the time to read the publication and then pick out something nice to say.

~

REJECTIONS

~

THE MAGAZINE of Fantasy and Science Fiction

"Thank you for giving me a chance to read "Farmyard Follies." I liked the quality of the prose and I thought this had an interesting hook, but in the end this story didn't quite win me over and I'm going to pass on it for Fantasy & Science Fiction. I wish you best of luck finding the right market for it and hope that you'll keep us in mind in the future.

Thanks also for mentioning Kelly Link's story -- I'm so glad you enjoyed it!"

~

ALLEGORY

"Thank you for sharing your story with us (and it's lovely to see another story of yours). This piece was really fun. I have a particular fondness for fancy poultry, and I love your voice here. I didn't think it was quite right for Allegory, though. It felt ... incomplete? It's hard to put this one into words. The way the birds took up instruments w/o much of a process--so easily and simply--made it feel too, for lack of a better word, easy. It might work better if the chickens have some time to brood over the potential for a terrible future fate and then, along the way, catch on to the notion of their musical potential. That would actually build up tension and it would make the formation of the band feel more believable (to whatever extent 4 chickens playing music can ever be believable, but you get my point)."

26

FARMYARD FOLLIES

Farmer Martin Ross sips his coffee but finds the flavour bitter. His brew always starts to taste nasty right around county fair time. Could envy affect your taste buds? Running a hand over his shaved grey head he tries not to think of his arch nemesis. He has a rivalry with his next door neighbour. Goose Creek is only a small steamy town in the Carolina Lowcountry, but they take their local fairs seriously. Joel Miller raises pygmy goats and trains a team of them to do a routine while he blows cues on a trumpet. While his long beard swings and his cowboy boots tap, the goats jump around in different formations and then end the act with a big pyramid, cute piled on top of cuter. Nobody can resist the four-legged cheerleaders, and Miller wins the talent contest at the local fair every year.

Ross runs a free-range chicken farm, and they sell the best eggs in the area. Happy chickens who get exposure to sunlight and lead a stress-free life produce eggs with thick yellow yolks, hard brown shells, and packed with Omega 3's. He has a Bantam rooster trained to run in circles around him, like a horse being lunged. It always gets a few laughs at the fair, but never the big win. He needs to find a chicken act that will leave Miller's drill team of nannies in the dust. With a sigh, Ross puts down his undrunk coffee and shrugs on his overalls. They hang loose on his thin frame, pounds lost to fair fretting. It's time to start his daily check-up of the fences and amount of grain in the silos. A new batch of laying hens came this morning and he wants to make sure everything is in good working order before he inspects them.

Meanwhile, it's chaos in the free-run chicken barn. The new arrivals are squawking and running amuck as they try to orient themselves. It may sound like just noise to the human ear, but the birds do have their own language.

"Where the cluck are we?" one girl shrieks.

"Get me the cluck out of here," another howls.

"That's my head you're standing on," comes from another.

Before today, they'd lived quietly in a small barn with only a few other chicks to avoid being squashed. Baby chicks are notorious for trampling each other. Talk about a life shock for them now. The large cover-all barn was almost wall-to-wall with hens and the noise deafening as new chickens collided with old birds. Dust shimmers in the sunlight as toes kick up sawdust and dried manure, making some of the old-timers cough and gag.

"Attention! All newcomers line up here. And we're not ducks, so no waddling! Get to it," a large black hen squawks above the ruckus.

Her voice thunders through the open space and everyone settles down. A group of four hens who'd been in the same shipping crate huddle together. They whisper among themselves, while the boss hen rounds up the more panicked stragglers.

"So what do sisters call yourselves? I'm Florence," a Red Sex-link bird says. She has lovely brown feathers and soft black eyes.

"I go by Mary," a cute Barred-Plymouth Rock says, "All four of us come from the same hatchery, but we can't be sisters being four different breeds," she puffs up her black and white foliage.

"Maybe we can be sisters by choice! Betty at your service here," a Columbian Rock with fine white feathers and mischievous grin joins in.

"Diana is my name," a Rhode Island Red says her eyes bright, not missing a thing, "this place is terrifying! I've never seen so many chickens in my life. What are there? Two hundred in here?"

Diana is interrupted by the boss hen hopping up on a large metal structure with multiple small boxes under it. Straw sticks out of each container, the odd egg, both brown and white, visible in some. She squawks for their attention.

"Welcome to the Ross Chicken Farm. I am the manager-on-the-floor and you can call me Barbara! You are all very lucky to live here. Most hens spend their lives in battery cages, but you are allowed to roam free and can even go outside for dust baths and sun bathing.

The four new friends look at each other in confusion. What is a battery cage?

"But there are rules here! You must lay your eggs in the laying berths. Do you see these little boxes I am standing on? You lay in here. Nowhere else. I catch you laying under the berths or in a corner, you will become soup!"

"Cluck me, Soup?" Florence says softly to Mary, "I guess that's a threat".

"Like we will have to make soup instead of eggs?" Betty asks.

"No," Mary says, "I think she means we will be the soup."

"That's ghastly!" Diana gasps.

"Silence, you cluckers!" she screams at the loud gaggle of four girls.

All the chickens freeze. A quiet settles over the barn with only the sound of the hanging feed dispensers creaking in the breeze.

"You will all lay at least one egg a day! No slackers here. If you stop laying, you will become soup," Barbara continues, "there is also a strict no fighting rule. No eye pecking, no feather pulling or else.... Soup!"

"Someone, somewhere, is eating a lot of soup." Betty whispers.

Barbara hops off the boxes and caws, "Follow me!"

All the new hens shuffle behind the large black bird as she starts pointing out the facilities. There are red waterers hanging from the ceiling on one side, while metal feeders hang down the other. The walls are taken up by the laying berths with big windows above them and the eggs roll down a ramp to an area under the barn. The most interesting part of the tour is the recreation area. There's a wall full of hay in a wired container for the girls to peck at, and kid's xylophones nailed to the wall. A few hens are bonking the different coloured keys with their beaks and random notes ring out.

"How long are we going to live here?" Mary asks, her cute puffy face creased in curiosity.

Barbara turns her dull body, the sheen of youth no longer on her feathers, and looks at the newbies, "The average stay is about a year, and when your egg production slacks off then it's time for..."

"Let me guess," Florence interrupts. "Soup!"

Some loud clucking, dust clouds, and random raining of feathers at one end of the barn distracts Barbara. It looks like too many chickens are trying to use the small door that leads to the outside pasture at the same time. As Barbara flaps off to check on the logjam, the girls look at one another.

"Well, I'm not sure how long a year is, but it doesn't sound long enough. What are we going to do when we stop laying eggs? Barbara is obviously older, what's her secret?" Betty frets.

Mary is distracted by the metal wiring on the hay dispenser and starts running her beak up and down it. She changes the rhythm and notes by strumming different length wires.

There is a reason these four chickens gravitated to one another. There is something special about all four of them. Not your average fowl.

Betty listens to the sound her friend is making, her white head cocked to one side as she nods to the beat. Then she starts flapping her wings right beside a metal feed container. As the strong bones hit the side of the metal, a low cool booming sound erupts.

Diana ruffles her red feathers in excitement and hops up to a xylophone. She pecks at the colored keys. Three short notes, three long ones. Something magical is happening to these impromptu instruments. The three girls manage to get their sounds in sync.

Florence hops up to another section of the hay wire and starts plucking with a toe, her harmony working perfectly with the others.

"I've been thinking about Barbara. I don't know how she avoids the soup pot, but I know one thing for sure," Florence opens her beak wide and goes from talking to singing, "there's no stopping us now. Now that we've found our way."

This has never happened before in this chicken barn. This has never happened before in any chicken barn anywhere else in the world. Florence, Mary, Betty, and Diana are pecking, singing, wing pounding and toe strumming like birds possessed. There is a joy and radiance around them that ushers in a new feeling of energy and possibility in the dusty barn. Every other chicken is silent and staring, beaks wide open, their red combs swaying to the beat. It is musical alchemy.

It's the four girl's luck that Farmer Ross walks in at that moment to check out his new flock. He drops his jaw in amazement listening to the catchy tune coming from the four different colored birds in the entertainment area. Then a slow smile crosses his face. An evil, delicious, delighted smile. Wait till Joel Miller sees what he is bringing to the local fair. Wait till everyone sees and hears! He is going to win the talent show for sure this year. In fact, he's pretty sure the local fair is only the beginning. These are some special birds. Time to pour a fresh cup of coffee, and Ross knows it will taste great.

ACKNOWLEDGMENTS

The speculative fiction market is full of talented authors, publishers and editors. I am amazed by how generous everyone involved in this anthology was with their time, advice and enthusiasm. This book never would have made it to print without the help of many.

Jonathan Lambert of Jolly Horror Press has been a mentor and most valuable resource on my journey into the world of comedy horror. When I was getting discouraged, he helped me craft a story that would work in his anthology and then gave it top spot. He also edited this entire manuscript, and answered all my newbie questions as I tried to figure out the self-publishing journey.

Thank you to Daniel Scott White of Mythaxis.com and Stuart Conover of horrortree.com for posting the full-length interviews of the publishers featured in *The Story Behind the Stories* on their respective websites.

Rong Hu is the talented graphic artist behind the cover design, and she created the artwork from scratch. This is also her first book cover.

Kristi Peterson Schoonover is the editor of 34 Orchard, and has gone above and beyond helping me refine my work.

Kimberly Fehr is an author herself, and I bothered her endlessly for advice and editing. She writes the quippiest copy and is relentless with her red pen.

Della Sullivan is my mother, also a writer of short stories, and she read every section over and over again, frequently telling me to "stop obsessing" when I needed to hear it. My sister, Lauren Sullivan, also served as a Beta reader and made sure any glaring spelling errors were taken care of. Paul Benoit, my brother, made sure the marketing messages were clear and catchy. Other friends and family who allowed me to bounce titles and ideas off them include Rachel Luttrell, Nella Ruprecht, Elena Poulos, Yvette Towrie, Jenny Psaltakis, Caterina Papadopoulos, Elaina Clarke, Cameron Sullivan, Amanda Sullivan, Gerry Benoit, Deb Benoit, and Sway Benoit.

Finally, I'd like to thank my husband and daughter for being supportive and allowing me to spend hours hunched over my computer without distraction.

ABOUT THE AUTHOR

Angelique Fawns is a journalist and speculative fiction writer. She began her career writing articles about naked cake dwellers in Tenerife, Canary Islands, and hosting a radio show in Mooloolaba, Australia. Now she works full-time making television commercials for Global TV in Toronto. She writes fiction for fun and uses her journalism skills to promote editors, publishers and authors. She lives on a farm north of the city with her husband, daughter, horses, goats, chickens, and a Potcake rescue dog.

ALSO BY ANGELIQUE FAWNS

If you liked *The Story Behind the Stories*, look for

The Publishers Behind the Pages

Featuring (to name a few)

Mannison Press

Third Flatiron Publishing

Mystery and Horror, LLC

The Great Void

Hawk & Cleaver

Jolly Horror Press

Impulsive Walrus

World Writers Collective

Plus many more rejection letters:

"We felt the gang violence gave the story a fan-fic feel"

"The piece made no sense"

"This always feels like it's on the edge of turning into a hot urban fantasy romance to me."

"How does the 'magic' work, and why isn't there a major investigation going on in a town where 50 some kids have gone missing?"

"Let's skip for a moment in the lack of plausibility... By the time the story seems to be going somewhere, the story ends."